THIS SHIT THE REALEST

Triple J's Story Part 3

THE EXECUTIVE HOMEBOY

Contents

Published by: The Executive Homeboy

This is a work of fiction. Names, characters, places and incidents either are products of the author's imagination or are used fictitiously. Any similarity to actual events or locales or persons, living or dead, is entirely coincidental.

Author Page

The Executive Homeboy is an award winning, Urban Novel Author with the natural gift of creative writing. He's the Chief Executive Officer of the Atlanta based investment company, Farm Houze Group LLC. For more information on the Author **visit:** **www.theexecutivehomeboy.com**

Synopsis

From the jailhouse to the A-house, James "Triple J" Johnson Jr. faces the fight of his life as he navigates the darkest corners of the state prison system. Labeled minimum-security by the computers, but caged with the state's most violent criminals, Triple J is thrown into chaos from day one.

Still, he plays it like a king. Armed with intelligence, charm, and those infamous "sexual superpowers," he even lays down game on a DOC sergeant during diagnostics.

After being shipped to the worst prison in the state, Triple J links up with his father's old friend, Stacks — a certified prison legend. Together, they dominate the contraband hustle: cell phones, smokes, designer fits, and more. But Triple J brings something new to the game — stock trading. With the help of The Executive Homies, the two start flipping dirty prison money into clean Wall Street profit.

Everything's smooth... until a familiar face from Triple J's past shows up on an online dating app. Against his better judgment, he lets her visit. The connection is real, the visit unforgettable — until tragedy strikes. A violent ambush leaves Stacks dead, and Triple J shattered.

Fueled by grief and vengeance, he digs deep to uncover who was behind it — but what he finds shakes everything he thought he knew. The answers lead him to a bloodline he never expected… and a destiny bigger than the streets.

First, it was *Shit Just Got Real.* Then, *Shit Just Got 2 Real.* Now, *This Shit the Realest.*

Prologue

*E*arly Thursday morning, James "Triple J" Johnson, Jr was awakened by the deputy knocking on the window of his Fulton Jail cell.

"Johnson, pack it up all the way. You're transferring," Deputy Pollard said with his baritone voice echoing throughout the sleeping dormitory.

Triple J, the ex-crime family boss, rose quickly to his feet.

It's time, he thought after his resting mind processed the deputies' words.

Triple J had been anxiously waiting for the day to come, after receiving five years for a jailhouse cellular phone, supposedly containing a picture of him inside. His defense team had already filed the appeal, knowing that bogus charge was a way for the state to get him in the system after his attorney's defeated the state in their RICO case.

"Say officer. Do I have enough time to take a quick shower?" Triple J asked humbly from inside of his cell.

"Yeah, I got ya," Deputy Pollard answered. "Tower, open cell 109," he continued.

Triple J grabbed his shower gear hanging from the edge of the top bunk. As he walked to the shower butterflies began to fill his stomach.

Damn, I'm really going to prison, he thought.

"Yoo, Triple J. You leaving?" One of the young guys asked from the cell above him.

"Yeah, I'm out of here," he replied, not really wanting to talk.

"If you can, fuck with me on some food, Big Bra," he said asking for Triple J's commissary items he couldn't take to prison with him.

"I got ya. Let me take care of my business first," Triple J replied.

After hanging his property on the curtain rail, he stepped in the shower and reality really set in. He'd been through a lot in life and like everyone else on their first time, he was nervous about going down the road.

"Whew," he sounded, letting out a heavy exhale. "Here you go James. You're headed to prison and it's no need to be nervous. You know how to handle yourself and you know you gotta make the best use of this time. Stop worrying man, you know the Pimp God will guide you. Look at it as five years, for you to work on you. Stay focused on the things that matter and own every moment for yourself and then The Executive Homies. They need you home, not gone. So, get yourself together. Walk with your head high and chest out," he said to himself before lifting his head and letting the warm water shower across his face.

In his heart, Triple J dreaded going to prison. He felt like he had failed those that depended on him, especially his sick father, James Jay. His jailhouse mule, Captain James had given him the ins and outs about prison, prepping him on what to expect for transfer day. To conceal his actual cell phone, he carved out a place in his 600-page discovery packet with a sharpened paperclip.

I gotta have my phone with me, he thought as he measured the spot.

With the extra net bag, used to wash his blue uniform, he quickly packed the commissary items and slung the bag over the top rail, landing it in front of his lil homie's cell.

"Preshate ya, Big Bra," the young guy said thanking him, as he watched the filled bag fall in front of his cell.

"It's all love. Y'all stay up," Triple J replied to the dormitory, now that he was ready to go.

He grabbed the two plastic mattresses from his bunk and drug them to the red zone, an area located at the front door. Next, he grabbed the net bag with his legal documents and dropped them on the day room table.

"You ready?" The tower officer asked after seeing him seated on the table.

"Yeah, I'm ready," Triple J replied, short of breath from the rapid movements.

A bead of sweat ran down the center of his back as rested.

"You gone be alright. Keep ya head up, King," the tower officer replied, still referring to him as the King Ape.

Most of the staff at Fulton Jail knew who Triple J was, especially those that worked his floor. They respected the ex-crime boss and many of them hated to see him go to prison, especially after the rest of his crew beat their charges.

"Preshate ya. I got it," Triple J replied to the tower officer as the dormitory door slid open.

Triple J grabbed his property bag and walked to the 700 zone.

"Okay, are you good to go? They just called for you downstairs," Deputy Pollard said after hanging the phone up.

"Yeah, I left my mats in the dorm. They're sitting by the door," Triple J said.

"Don't worry about that. We'll get Big Will to grab it," the deputy replied, referring to the hallway orderly.

He handcuffed Triple J's hands to the front and escorted him downstairs assisting him with his bags. Downstairs, the transfer deputy stood in front of the holding cell as he waited for them.

"Johnson, what's your JID number," the deputy asked looking at his transfer paperwork once they approached.

"1526182," Triple J replied.

"Okay, change into this," he said, handing Triple J a folded blue suicide jumpsuit.

Damn, this is degrading, he thought as he stripped down to his T-shirt, boxers and socks.

The deputy then grabbed the handcuffs and shackles and put them on him. Walking to the sally port, Triple J struggled as the uncomfortable shackles rubbed against the inside of his ankle.

"You good?" The deputy asked, seeing how slow he was walking.

"Hell naw, this shit hurts," he replied, lifting his head high as he suffered in pain.

"They ain't that bad, you'll be good. We're almost to the car," the deputy replied.

Let me put this shit on you, then tell me how they feel, Triple J thoughts as he struggles to keep his cool.

Outside of the sliding doors, was a waiting black Charger with green writing on the side.

"Alright, watch ya head," the deputy said after opening the rear passenger door.

Triple J had already shown difficulties walking and struggled to balance himself as he got into the car. With no assistance from the deputy, he wobbled several times before finally finding his balance to get his foot inside.

"Not Triple J the King Ape," said the young deputy seated in the driver's seat.

Triple J looked at him through the mirror but didn't recognize him as an officer from the floor.

"I see the name on the paperwork, but I ain't know it was you," he continued.

Triple J nodded his head with a slight smile, before laying his head on the car window. Going to prison was depressing and there was nothing he preferred more than peace and quiet, at the time.

"8827 to radio, I have one inmate leaving Fulton Jail to prison diagnostics. My mileage is 110346, 10-4."

After the dispatcher repeated his words, the car fired out before they pulled out.

As they started their journey one of the deputies turned on the radio. Just as Triple J's mind began to race, the morning show host came on.

"Good morning, Atlanta," he began his daily devotional with a low instrumental playing in the background. "Today is Thursday, December 7th, 2017, and this is Lil B with your Morning Message. We're living in some very trying times and for some of us it's rougher than it is for others.

The thing we have to remember is that God gives his toughest battles to his strongest warriors. I have a good friend of mine who's incarcerated and he's been tried, tried and tried again. I don't know if he's listening right now, but if you are Triple J, I want you to know that Atlanta loves you and we're praying that God continues to bless you and guide you along your journey," he said before the spiritual music began to play.

As Triple J listened to his words, he knew the song was what he needed.

"This is not a punishment, this is an assignment," said the voice of his ancestors.

Relaxed in thought, Triple J dozed off as they traveled down the highway. He was awakened as the car slowed, and knew they'd reached their destination. Layers of barbed wire fencing and tall white towers surrounded, prison diagnostics and the heavy force of negative energy could be felt on the outside. Triple J knew right then that, *This Shit the Realest.*

Chapter One

*a*s they pull onto the concrete lot, Triple J sees vehicles parked from different state law enforcement agencies. Vans, cars and buses, all used for prisoner transport. The sheriff deputies waste no time getting him out and marching him across the transport yard. Triple J saw that most of the prisoners were already in the state system, wearing white uniforms with blue stripes along the side of their pants.

Butterflies filled the stomach of the ex-crime boss as he passed a man badly beaten with two black eyes.

"I don't know what his hand game look like, but his duck game was on zero," another transferring prisoner said, making a joke of the man.

As they neared the prison, Triple J saw that there was a railing system in place similar to an amusement park.

Damn, this shit looks like a modern-day slave movie, he thought as the deputy escorted him through.

Once they reached the other waiting prisoners, the transfer deputy removed Triple J's handcuffs and shackles.

Leaving him in the line with other waiting intake prisoners, the deputy walked to a brown podium where a state officer stood in a black corrections jacket. Triple J watched as the deputy handed over a manila envelope to the black, burly and bald corrections officer.

"Take care of yourself," the deputy said, tapping Triple J's shoulder before leaving him with the others.

Ain't no more county jail, he thought as the deputy walked away.

Waiting in line with the other intake prisoners, a large group filed behind him from other counties. Many of them were of different ethnicities and ages and Triple J was confused as to why they were wearing regular clothes.

They got me here looking like a psych patient, when everybody else wearing the clothes, they got locked up in, he said to himself.

Triple J's mind raced with thoughts as he stood in line.

"Have you been here before?" A frail voice behind him asked.

Triple J was looking around checking out his surroundings before he looked at the man that had spoken.

Short, white and light weight, you gone have it hard, Triple J thought as he quickly analyzed him.

From the frantic look in his eyes and the question he'd asked, Triple J could tell the young man was afraid. It was Triple J's first time in prison, and he didn't know what to tell him.

"Naw, this my first time. You might wanna check in," he said, giving him the best advice that he could.

"Check in?" The young man asked with a confused look on his face.

"Yeah, check-in. Tell the first officer that you see that

you fear for your life and you wanna go to the box," Triple J said to him.

At Fulton Jail, there weren't any white's on the 7th floor, not even the officers. Someone like him would have been terrorized, day and night without a shadow of thought, first because of his skin color and second because he was scary. Triple J had never been to prison, but based on the horror stories he'd heard about prison diagnostics, it was going to be hard for the little white fella if he didn't check in.

"Gentleman, Welcome to prison diagnostics," the officer behind the podium said, speaking to the group. "When I call your name, you will be given a number. Remember this number because it's how you'll be identified throughout the day. Once you get your number, you're going to call it back to me before you step through this red door. In there, you'll be given further instructions by the officers inside," he said pointing with his right hand in the direction of the door.

Several names were called before, Triple J's.

"Johnson! James Johnson, Jr. Your number is 9," he said, pointing Triple J to the red door. "What's your number?" He asked before Triple J entered.

"My number is 9," Triple J said before stepping inside.

Two men, both tactically dressed in black uniforms, stood at the front of the room.

Damn, here we go again with this clown shit again, Triple J thought as soon as he saw them.

"Give that bag to the officer in the window. Strip and put everything you're wearing in the gray bin shower shoes too," one of them said.

Like the see through suicide suit wasn't already degrading, Triple J stripped down out of all of his clothes like he was told. Being told by another man that he had to stand nude was his biggest hatred towards incarceration, especially now.

Standing on the black footprints, how he did when he came into the world, Triple J's feet froze from the freezing tile floor.

"Gentleman, welcome to Georgia's prison diagnostics," the CERT Officer began to speak once the room was filled. "The first thing, I want to make clear, is that this is a hands-on facility and we have zero tolerance here. I don't care about your gang affiliations or what you did in the county. This is my shit and once you think you running my shit, I'll be there to bless you with the hands of God," the CERT Officer said, holding his right hand in the air. "I give respect, and I demand mines. The women you see that work here or volunteer all belong to me. If you disrespect them, you're disrespecting me and at that time you'll be blessed by the hands of God," he continued holding his right hand in the air. "When my staff speak to you, it's Ma'am yes ma'am and Sir yes sir. Do you understand?"

"Sir yes sir," the group answered.

"Do you understand?" He asked again.

"Sir yes sir," the group answered louder.

"When you're passing an officer or any other staff member, you will stop walking and say ma'am moving ma'am or sir moving sir. Do you understand?" He asked.

"Sir yes sir," the group answered.

"Do you understand?" He asked again.

"Sir yes sir," the group answered louder.

"Passing me or any other staff member without permission, will be taken as disrespect and you will be blessed by the hands of God. Do you understand?" He asked.

"Sir yes sir," the group answered.

The CERT officer then grabbed a white container with a sprayer attached to a black hose.

"First four lets' go," he said, spraying the men with the liquid substance inside the container before directing them to the showers.

This is so degrading, Triple J thought as the officer sprayed his face and body down with the mystery liquid.

"Gone in there," he continued, staring at Triple J with a menacing look in his eyes.

You don't want this shit Toy Soldier, Triple J thought as he passed.

With his bare hands he quickly showered with no washcloth, moving fast to rinse the liquid off his body.

Five years of this shit. Don't know how I'm going to do it, he thought trying to relax despite the depression he faced.

After exiting the other side of the shower, he walked to the property window.

"What size shoes do you wear?" The inmate worker asked him.

"10 in a half," Triple J replied.

"We don't have half sizes," the inmate worker continued, handing Triple J a size 11 boot.

They were old and broke down, but they were shoes. Triple J was thankful for them because in the county everyone had to wear white shower shoes and fight barefooted like ancient African warriors.

After getting the boots, he was issued a white net bag with several items inside. Triple J fished through their first for the clothing items. The uniform pants he grabbed had a huge hole in the crotch area and the supposedly white t-shirts were brown like someone had done construction in them.

"They gave me somebody else shit to put on," he said to himself, angrier at the situation, more than he was before.

Quickly he dressed himself and waited for the next steps.

Everyone entering prison diagnostics were forced to cut all of the hair on their heads for their initial pictures. Waiting for them were several inmate barbers wearing white barber jackets and they had one haircut, all of it off.

"Next man," one of them called out.

Triple J stood and went to his chair. Without a word he flipped on the clippers and against the grain he went, shaving the ex-crime boss's head. For his initial mugshot he was left with a mustache only.

Damn, he just cut my waves out, Triple J thought after the cut was done and he'd be given his prison identification card.

"Hold on," he said, turning back to the officer that took his picture. "This ain't right. I'm not a sex offender," he said with a confused look on his face.

"I know who you are and that's not what that means," she said laughing at him. "We refer to everyone as offenders in the state now. Someone filed a lawsuit saying that being called a prisoner or inmate is a form of cruel and unusual punishment," she continued laughing at him.

"Hell naw," he replied, laughing with her after letting out a slight exhale.

Sargent Washington, a prison veteran that's been in the system for twelve years. Everyone that entered the state's prison system within the last decade had crossed paths with her in some way at prison diagnostics.

For most of the new intakes, Sargent Washington was the sexiest woman they'd ever seen in real life. Cute redbone with naturally long hair, she was an American man's dream girl. She was the biggest woman crush, to the chain gang inmates and officers. She knew that everyone liked her, but for the first time the tables had turned. As Triple J walked away, she bit down on her bottom lip, turned on by the dominant thug demeanor the ex-crime boss displayed.

"Johnson!" She called out stopping him before he entered the gym. "Tomorrow I'm gone see about getting you on my detail," she said, with a strong sexual desire in her eyes.

"Have a good day ma'am," Triple J quickly replied before walking off.

I ain't fucking with these stupid ass niggas, he thought as he walked off, remembering the speech the CERT Officer had just given him about the prison woman. *And they work in the same area. Hell naw,* he continued in thought.

Inside of the gymnasium, men from all over the state sat quietly. Like every other facility for incarcerated men, the first step was to be screened and cleared by Medical and mental health professionals, before going to the housing areas.

"A Boy! I remember you," a heavyset black guy yelled across the gymnasium. "Ain't you White Boy Billy?" he asked.

Everyone's eyes followed him to see who he was talking to.

"You don't know me, Boy!" White Boy Billy spat back in a heavy southern drawl.

"Smith State Prison. You owed me $400 for a cap of cream. Yo bitch ass ran to the box and sent the folks at me. You Rat!" The black guy replied.

White Boy Billy was surrounded by several of his brothers from the Southern Kracker Klan, a prison gang that started in Cobb County Jail.

"What's he talking about Krack?" One of them asked.

"I don't know that man," White Boy Billy replied.

"That man just called you a rat. You gotta fix ya face Krack," another one said to him.

Immediately, White Boy Billy stood up and walked towards the black guy who stood by the exit door. Quickly closing the distance between them he charged the black guy with a wild right hook. Missing with the wild blow, he was punched in the stomach twice before a hard blow was delivered to his right side of White Boy Billy's temple area.

Falling in a twisted motion backwards, White Boy Billy banged his head on the edge of the steel bench and the hard thump echoed throughout the room leaving the onlookers in total shock.

No one knew at the time but at that very moment, the new arrivals had just witnessed their first prison homicide.

Immediately after the fight, Triple J grabbed the tongue of his boots and pulled his strings tighter.

This Shit the Realest.

Chapter Two

A-House, also known by its moniker Animal House was where Triple J and two other new arrivals were escorted for housing. No one wanted to go into A-House because of its reputation for extreme violence. As soon as the new crew walked in, several gangs surrounded them.

"New arrivals," several of them yelled as they walked in.

Triple J realized it was a call for the others, and he prepared himself for the trouble to come.

"What y'all got?" One of the guys closest to them asked. "I need some new boots too," another one said, looking at Triple J.

Keeping a stern look in his eyes the ex-crime boss laughed at them on the inside because they had no idea what they were up against.

"Y'all act like animals, but I see you're horrible at picking your prey," Triple J said before chopping the last guy to walk towards him in the throat with lightning speed.

Shocked and surprised, he fell to his knees while

holding his throat gasping for air. Triple J knocked him flat to the floor with a roundhouse kick to the side of his head. Immediately, the others stepped back all in shock by the black ninja.

"I don't know how you lil niggas get down in here, but unless you're ready to dance with the devil, I advise you stay the fuck out of my way," Triple J said looking into the eyes of every one of them before walking to range five where the officer said his cell was.

The entire housing unit was silent as he moved, and all of the troublemakers knew they didn't want any smoke with the new man.

In the front of his mind, Triple J wished more would have come so he could make more examples, just to let them know shit could get real, but his respect for the art held him a bay.

The greatest fight is the fight you'll never have to fight; he remembered his martial arts instructor telling him.

Prison diagnostics had a different setup than the county jail. A-House had eight ranges, and his cell was on range five located downstairs in the far back. When Triple J entered, he saw that the cell had a wooden box attached to the right wall and that's where his property was to be stored. Behind the property box was the toilet and sink, located on the rear wall. Built in the early 60's, prison diagnostics still had sliding cell bars like in the old prison movies.

In the county jail, the cells were closed in, and the toilet was in the front not the back of the cell. The bed was on the back wall and not the side wall. It's less room in here but I'm gone have to make it work, he thought of processing his space for combat.

After setting down his property, Triple J stepped to his

cell door and looked around. An older bare mouth black man stepped out of the cell next to Triple J's.

"I'll clean up your cell for a soup," he said to Triple J.

"I ain't been to commissary yet, Unk. But if you take care of the cell for me, I promise I'll make sure you straight while I'm here," Triple J said to him.

"Another one of y'all I got you niggas," the old man said to Triple J. "The last nigga that was in the cell that you're in sleeps in the infirmary now with a wired jaw because he didn't wanna pay me," he said before returning to his cell.

At the time, Triple J wished he had a soup for the old man because his cell smelled awful. As he searched the room his eyes went to the white towel covering the stainless-steel toilet. Once he lifted the towel, the stench screamed across the cell and into the hallway. Bil from the last occupants was left inside as an unflushed gift.

I gotta get out of this shit, Triple J said to himself as he looked around. *Prison is no place for a playa, but it's something I gotta do,* he reminded himself.

Triple J walked around A-House by himself until he found the orderly. He asked him for some chemicals and gloves and tackled the smell inside.

The earlier transfer had taken his energy. He went to sleep with his boots on just in case an unexpected visitor decided to come through while he was asleep.

The next morning after breakfast, he was awakened by the dorm guys going crazy.

"Big Booty Sarge on the floor y'all," one of the guys yelled.

"Baby Mama! When you gone let me work your detail?" another one yelled from his cell.

She ignored them all because on that day she had one man on her mind.

"Johnson!" she called out. "Johnson what cell are you in?"

"Which one?" Asked a guy on the top tier.

"James Johnson," she then said.

"Triple J! The officer calling for you," the orderly said, pushing a dust mop across the floor.

Triple J knew the call was for him when he saw what officer was calling for him, but he ignored her. When she called out his name the second time he answered.

"Triple J, what cell are you in," she asked.

If she knows I'm in A-House then she knows what cell I'm in, he thought.

But going along with her game he answered.

"125," he answered through the prison bars.

His cell door opened, and he stepped out shirtless, showing off his chiseled chest and abdomen. Since coming out of the coma, Triple J made it his business to get back in good shape especially since he was going to prison. The physical therapy and two a day workouts put him right where he needed to be, magazine ready and Sargent Washington liked it.

"I need your help. Please put on a shirt and come with me," she said, staring at him.

After putting on his shirt he stepped back out of his cell, and she closed it back.

"I told you I was gone get you on my detail," she said as he walked towards her.

"You did and I laughed because the judge ain't sentenced me to labor. I got sentenced to do time," he continued.

"Boy shut up and bring ya ass on," she replied, slapping him on the arm.

They both exchanged laughs and quickly paused. There was a strong sexual charge between the two and they both felt it.

She ain't the baddest bitch in the world, but got damn she's thick, he thought as they walked down the hall.

Sargent Washington stood 5"11 and weighed around 240lbs. She had a small baby pouch but compared to her backside it was flatter than a sheet of paper. Her uniform pants were filled with her well-rounded attention grabber and thighs; Triple J couldn't resist looking at her as they walked.

She knows exactly what she's doing, he said to himself.

The intake area he entered at prison diagnostics was her area. Outside of the Tuesday and Thursday transfers, she usually sat there alone. One of the CERT team officers liked her and he sometimes stopped by, but other than that she sat alone. She knew Triple J was the made man the news made him out to be and getting him on her detail was important because he could give her the company she truly yearned for.

"I'm going to give you a spray bottle with bleach inside. All I want you to do is spray the tables and wipe it up. Sometimes we get a few deliveries. It's nothing but a few boxes, we'll sort them out and I'll take you outside to throw them away," she said when they entered.

"So, you think I'm a janitor?" Triple J asked.

"No, it's called custodial maintenance," she replied, correcting him.

"I ain't gone lie Sarge," Triple J said, looking around the

room. "You're cool but this ain't what I do. I don't even clean my own house, I have maids."

She walked to a maintenance closet and Triple J followed her. Quickly she turned about face and pulled him close to her.

"Well clean me up?" She asked before kissing the stunned Triple J on the lips. "I need you to fuck me really good, King Ape," she said as her eyes rolled into the back of her head.

What's up with these women and all this aggressive shit, he thought as she held him.

Sargent Washington knew what he needed to get right. She grabbed his hand and placed it on her pillow soft ass.

I'm finna fuck the shit out of this bitch, he thought as he began to kiss her back.

Breaking their kiss, she looked at him with caution.

"I know I'm being a Ho right now, but please don't tell on me," she said looking at him with caution.

Although he was the ex-crime boss he still stood on principles.

"Omerta," he replied, the mafia's code of silence.

Sargent Washington knew it was against federal law, having sexual relations with an inmate, but felt so comfortable with him.

Losing her belt, she pulled down her pants and Triple J grabbed her around the waist. Slightly raising her from the floor he sat her laced covered ass on the mop sink.

Damn, I done fucked in so weird places since I been locked up. First it was the airplane bathroom and now the mop sink, he laughed at himself in thought.

Triple J dropped to his knees and slid her panties to the side exposing her phat vagina lips. Like she was all his he lifted her legs onto his shoulders and began to have his way with her entirely.

"Hiss," Sargent Washington exhaled from the warm and wet tongue vibrating on her clitoris.

It had been a while since he'd pleased a woman outside of his wife with the oral pleasure. Since their official break up he'd yearn for some pussy pie and sarge was the lucky woman.

Sargent Washington struggled to keep the noise down, but the tongue tricks Triple J did had her legs shaking and noise making. He slurped and rolled his tongue around on her swollen clitoris, making her whole body vibrate uncontrollably.

"Oh fuck," she screamed as her eyes rolled to the back of her head. "You do better than my rose," she said, referring to her sex toy.

Triple J knew he was gifted, forcing her hips to roll on his face. He pleased her with his tongue until she came, letting her juices squirt all over his face.

"You said you wanted to be cleaned up," he said as he stood up.

Together they stood to their feet. Triple J turned her around and bent her over the mop sink. He squatted down and spread her ass part before licking her brown booty hole.

"I'm about to cum again," she screamed as he ate her ass.

This was his first time licking ass, but he did it like he was a veteran. He continued to go crazy reading her body as he flowed.

"Will you please just fuck me," she begged in between moans.

"I thought you wanted me to clean up," he replied, being sarcastic.

"You trying to make me fall in love with you," she said. " Now please fuck me," she continued.

Triple J knew his dick game was phenomenal, and she would be hooked like fish. Being as gentle as he could, he inserted his well girthed rod into her hot and ready pussy pie. Immediately, her arms were swinging around the closet as she reached for a place to brace herself.

"Oh shit," she screamed, eyes bucked and back arched.

"You asked for this dick, you big booty bitch. Now stop running," he said viciously, biting his bottom lip as he piped her.

Struggling to hold back her screams, Sargent Washington grabbed a handful of her shirt and bit down on it.

"I'm so-orry, I'm so-orry, I'm sorry," she screamed while biting down on her shirt.

"Bitch you know this pussy mines now," he said aggressively as he stabbed her from the back.

"This is yo pussy daddy. I pro-mise this is yo pu-uh-uh-ssy,' she continued to cry in between strokes.

Triple J had no letup in his body, giving her everything that she'd ask for.

"You asked for this dick now take it," he said when she put her hand back trying to stop him. "Take it," he continued, grabbing her hands and pulling her to him.

She screamed in pleasurable pain as he continued to fuck her. Slapping her ass like a slut he made her pussy squeeze every time he slapped her.

"I'm about to come," he said as his erection got harder.

"Cum in my mouth. Cum in my mouth," she said in response.

She turned quickly and dropped to her knees. Before she could open her mouth, Triple J released his heavy load, ejaculating all over her face. She sat there speechless with a shocked look on her face. Before pulling up his pants he looked at her cum covered face.

"I don't know who the fuck you thought I was, but *This Shit the Realest.*"

Chapter Three

*S*tabbings, extortion, rape and other gang violence was regular at prison diagnostics, but no judge had sentenced them to such. Several prisoners had filed lawsuits for cruel and unusual punishment, leading the DOJ to open an investigation, but that didn't change a thing.

"There is no way I could get use to living like a savage," Triple J said pertaining to his living conditions in A-House.

It didn't take long for the ex-crime boss to take control. Within a two-week period, Triple J had a small army built around him. They were ordained to maintain law and order inside of A-House correcting anyone that got out of pocket.

The prison was supposed to have their CERT team, Corrections Emergency Response Team, for such a job, but they were scared of A-House. Triple J's HURT team, a group of eight lifers, were about that life and ready to HURT anybody that brought unwanted attention to the renowned Triple J's A-House.

Without Sargent Washington breaking the law, he

would have never been able to keep them cool. Utilizing her personal team of corrupt staff members, Triple J made sure he and his Hurt team eaten good. Every meal came from the free world and never did they eat a state tray. Not even on chicken day.

Like in the county jail, Triple J got multiple deliveries of contraband phones and drugs through their network, giving all of the young wild hitters the things they needed to cool out.

"What's going on in A-House? Y'all been chill over here," the warden said once during inspection.

There were minor altercations with the new arrivals, but nothing serious enough for staff involvement and they loved that.

"I see y'all chain gang in here, so I'm gone let the chain gang run itself as there was no deaths," the warden said.

"Triple J you have a call-out," the officer said as he stood in front of Triple J's cell.

The ex-crime boss was reading off his phone when the officer called his name. Already with the best gear, Triple J stood up and slid his sock covered feet into his brand name slides. Triple J knew he had completed the diagnostics process and as he walked to the cell door he was in total confusion for why he would be getting a call out now.

"Warden!" He read aloud before looking at the officer.

The call-out was for 9:15am, two hours from the time on his digital watch.

"What is this about?" He wondered as he paced back and forth in his cell.

One of these nigga's might've said some, he thought about his illegal activity. *Hell naw. They would have ran down on me or locked one of my officers up,* he continued quickly dismissing the negative thought.

Since the death penalty case was dismissed, Triple J promised to never worry himself again.

As he got himself together for his call-out, time flew by. Before he'd realized, it was time to take that walk.

"Second session callouts only. Second session call out's," the officer yelled as he walked through A-House.

"Big bra you got a call out?" One of his Hurt team hitters asked.

"Yeah," Triple J answered as he put on his designer glasses.

"Do you want one of us to walk with you?" He continued.

"Naw, I'm good. Going to see the Warden," Triple J replied.

"Ha! What y'all finna have some executive meeting or some?" he said jokingly.

Triple J didn't reply, only giving him a slight chuckle. His mind was still racing in thought as he walked out of A-House.

Why is he calling me up here? He continued to question.

The warden's office was no place he'd ever been to or planned on going to. Assuming it was somewhere in the front, he walked towards medical, the area he saw officers exiting with their bags.

Once reaching the yellow bars, he spoke to the officer in the control booth.

"I'm not sure where I'm supposed to go ma'am, but I have a Warden's call-out," he said, holding up the paper slip.

"Johnson?" she asked through the intercom speaker.

"Yes ma'am," Triple J replied.

"Have a seat on that bench. I'm gonna let him know you're out here," she said smiling with her light green braces.

Triple J smiled back at her thinking to himself; *she has to be the prettiest woman that works here.*

She had sun kissed brown skin, with long natural black hair. She didn't have on any make-up, nor lashes but the gloss on her bubblegum filled lips was enough to capture his eye.

"You can go have a seat na," she said, speaking in her southern girl accent. "The warden will be with you in a minute," she continued breaking his stare with her smile.

Damn! Lil Baby, he thought, loving the view.

Seated only a few feet away from the booth, Triple J couldn't help but to eye fuck her.

"You know I see you right," she said with a huge smile spreading across her face.

"I want you to," he replied, making her smile spread further.

They both felt an attraction for one another, but Triple J was locked in with Sargent Washington. She was his get money girl.

"What are you doing out here?" One of the tactically dressed CERT officers asked with aggression in his voice.

"I have a call-out to see the warden," Triple J answered him.

Without saying a word, the CERT officer walked off. The way he pushed off, Triple J knew the only reason he stopped was to show his authority in front of the attractive female officer.

"This clown as nigga, is a real chili pimp. He claims

these his hoes, but don't even know the rules to the game," he said to himself.

"If a hoe chooses on another pimp, it's law that you let her choose and be cool about it," Sir Lowe, a pimp from Grant Park said to him when he was young.

"I gotta get out of this shit," Triple J said laughing off the situation.

"Mr. Johnson," the officer from the booth called from a door behind him. "The warden's ready to see you," she continued.

Butterflies filled his gut as he stood and walked towards her.

"You're not in trouble, if that's what you're thinking," she said, putting him at ease.

Inside the control booth he was only able to view her top half. As she stood in the doorway to the warden's hallway, he viewed the total package, and her bottom half was immaculate. Perfectly curved with an itty-bitty waistline, she captured all eyes with her athletic thick thighs.

"What do you run in the 40?" Triple J asked, assuming she ran track.

"Ahh man! I don't know now. My last time on the clock it was like a 4.8," she replied humbly.

4.8! Damn that's fast, he thought.

"I'll hate for a nigga to escape and you chasing his ass," Triple J replied being a flirt.

"I ain't chasing nobody, but you." she continued, eyes fluttering at him.

Triple J smiled because he knew that she was dead serious. All of the lady corrections officers wanted a shot at the ex-crime boss and now that he knew she was in pursuit he vowed not to make her chase long.

"Okay then Cute Trooper," he replied with a chuckle.

"It's Trooper Parham in Hot Pursuit," she said jokingly into her shoulder mic.

Triple J had a fly reply but before he could they were outside of the Warden's office.

Officer Parham knocked at his door, getting a quick reply.

"Mr. Johnson. Please come in," he said standing from his desk.

Warden Jones was the youngest prison warden in the state's system. Only thirty-four years young, he surprised many with his youthful face the first-time people saw him. Although he and Triple J had never spoken directly, they had a lot in common.

"What up, Mr. Johnson. We've never met, I'm Warden Keondre Jones," he said, extending his hand to Triple J for a handshake. "I've been in the system for sixteen years now and I have to admit you are the highest profile prisoner I've ever seen in the state system. I was looking at your scribe before you came in here and you don't even have a violent conviction. To be honest, you're actually one of the best prisoners, I've ever had under my watch," he said opening up the conversation with Triple J. "I called you here today because I've been wondering, how is it that A-House has been the worst housing unit since I've been in the system and now there hasn't been one 10/10 reported in the last two months?" He asked.

Triple J stared at the warden in silence, as his mind wondered what he was trying to get to.

"I apologize, Mr. Johnson. I'm not trying to scare you, but you've been a huge blessing to this prison. Initially, we were concerned with you being in A-House. There were talks amongst the administration that you may be in danger there, but you've changed the whole atmosphere. I called you here today to say, thank you," Warden Jones said.

As he spoke thoughts continued to race through Triple J's mind. Breaking the awkward silence, he replied to the trying too hard to be cool warden.

"I'm not sure who you think I am sir, but A-House is only where I was assigned a cell. Anything else that's happening there has nothing to do with me," Triple J replied with a straight face.

Triple J wanted no credit for what was happening in A-House. That kind of recognition would make him a prison puppet with the administration. All he wanted was to do his time under the radar as quietly as possible.

"I know better, and I like your response," Warden Jones replied, staring at Triple J. "Okay, well yesterday I received a call from the Fulton Jail. The officer that was arrested in your case will be transferring here today. If there's a problem, please let me know, I can arrange for you to be put in protective custody," Warden Jones said.

Triple J stared at him for several seconds as he searched for the best words to reply with.

"I viewed you as a man of intelligence. With all due respect Warden, I came here with five years for a cell phone. Y'all put me in the worst housing unit around all of the lifers in the state and now you call me up here to insult me. You got an ex-cop coming to prison, but you think I should be in protective custody. Listen to me, Warden Sir," Triple J said, getting close to him. "Now you know who I am. And you know what I'm capable of. Please don't ever call me up here again to rub shit in my face," Triple J replied with a murderous look in his eyes.

Although he kept a straight face, the heavy gulp in his throat was enough for Triple J to know that he understood.

"For future references, help the bear because I don't need none," Triple J continued before turning to walk out of the warden's office.

This Shit the Realest.

Chapter Four

Shipping days were the most chaotic times at prison diagnostics, especially in the early hours. Corrections officers raced around the compound for offender transfers packing them up and dressing them out. Most of the offenders in A-House were classified as close security and had a good idea of where they were going, a level 5 prison.

"Big Homie where you think they are sending you to?" Lil Hot, one of the young guys that looked up to him asked.

"I have no idea lil brother. My best guess is another prison," Triple J replied sarcastically in a humble tone.

Some people just wanted to talk even if it wasn't about nothing, Triple J realized during his time incarcerated.

There were so many places he learned a man can go after prison diagnostics from state prisons, private prisons and county camps. Some people back on parole violations were eligible for the Transitional Centers, but that wasn't the case for Triple J, so his best guess was another prison.

"I hope I go to a county camp. I ain't trying to go nowhere that bih biting at," he continued.

"My best wishes to you lil brother. Whatever the outcome is, find a way to make the best of it," Triple J said to him.

"Most definitely," Lil Hot replied.

"Prisons are a gold mine and I'm not referring to the illegal activity. The minds of the people inside without distractions is what makes it Golden. We're here with some of the smartest people in the world that did something dumb," Triple J said, trying to give him a little game.

"What that mean?" He asked, interrupting Triple J.

"Most people get locked up and correct themselves and their outlook on life by reading books like, "*Think and Grow Rich*" by Napoleon Hill and "*48 Laws of Power,*" by Robert Green. Those types of books gas the flames inside of us and put us in that Golden state of thinking," Triple J continued.

"Oh okay! I understand what you're saying now. People in prison did some dumb shit to get locked up, but they start reading books and learn a new way of thinking," Lil Hot replied.

"That's half right. There are doctors, lawyers and police detectives in prison," Triple J said thinking about the famous detective that got locked up on his case. "Society sees them as some of the most educated individuals, but still they end up in here with us because of the dumb shit they did," Triple J continued.

Triple J had captured the eyes and ears of a small group seated around him. Several of the guys nodded their heads in agreement as he spoke.

"Listen to me, guys. Everywhere you go, you'll see at

least three ways to make a million dollars. Use this time to learn and understand business and its laws. Educate yourselves on basics of contracts, stocks, bonds and credit. Focus your mind on becoming your own boss. Even if you don't learn the game so well that major companies offer to pay you seven and eight figures a year sitting on their executive's board. We need more executive homies," Triple J replied.

"Where do you say I should start?" Lil Hot asked.

"Great question. Since we're in here I think you should start in the library. The law library should have books and cases on business especially, employment law. You should see things like the equal opportunity act, contract agreements and corporations. You can write the Secretary of State office and request documents on LLC's and S-Corps. They should respond with applications and instructions on how to fill them out," Triple J paused in thought. "Also look up information on business structure, Articles of Incorporations and taxes. So many people with money get in trouble for not paying their state and federal taxes," he continued.

One of the older guys that was listening interrupted him with a question.

"Excuse me, Sorry for getting in y'all conversation," he said respectfully.

"You good? What's up Unk?" Triple J asked.

"I like what you doing, dropping useful jewels on the young brothers. You speak very well like a college professor or something," he said, patronizing the businessman. "Last year, I was left my parents' estates after my mom went on to glory. I can't seem to get help from the trustee they assigned over the trust money while I'm locked up. What do you suggest I do?" The old man asked.

"To be honest big brother, that's a question for an attorney. You can write the State Bar and request a list of trust attorneys to get some legal help," Triple J says, pausing at the look of defeat on his face. "I'm not sure what you're trying to do with the estate but depending on the way your parents structured the trust, your trustee may only act as they requested," Triple J continued.

"I understand, but when I was trying to use the house as collateral to bond out, she told me I couldn't. It's my house, why can't I use my house to bond myself out?" He asked.

"That's something you have to ask an attorney, Big Brother. I actually have an irrevocable trust over my estate. There are several ways of structuring them. Right now, everything is left to my father unless I change it," Triple J continued.

"I'm just saying, it's all some bullshit," The old man said. "What ever happen to when they die you get everything left to you, without the red tape?"

"I apologize but that's the best advice I have for you Big Brother. I still say you should speak with an attorney," Triple J continued.

Everyone in prison has a different story. Some were ludicrous and others were heart felt. Triple J felt he'd found his purpose to help those in need.

After hearing the pain in the old man's voice, he couldn't help but feel sympathetic towards him. Triple J knew the justice system was all about the Benjamins and had the old man been able to use his family's home as collateral, his chances of being in prison would've been much slimmer.

Several uniformed officers wearing black bulletproof vests with CORRECTIONS stitched across the front entered the room.

"Gentleman, if I call your name, I need you to stand and come with me," one of them said.

The room was completely silent as everybody listened in agony.

"Tyrone Avery, Derrick Beasley, Antonio Collier, Oscar Henry, and James Johnson. Y'all coming with me," he continued.

"Y'all be good," Triple J said as he stood up and slid out of the group.

"You to Big Homie," the old man replied, causing an eruption of laughter amongst the group.

Since two correctional officers were killed during transfer, no one knew where they were going until they got on the bus.

As they were waiting to cross the prison yard, the guy directly behind him started rapping.

"I had a dream I was staying in a million-dollar house, in
the middle of a million-dollar trap,
Woke up, officer at the gate with a turnkey, chow call
dropping my trap on the flap.
In my dream I was a king wit a plate full of steak, now I'm
staring at an oatmeal tray.
Aladdin, I need me a genie to grant me a wish and get me
up and out of this place,
Mama, Mama, can't you see, what these folks did to me,
They cut all my hair and gave me a bald head, with GDCP
pressed on some orange pants,
ID card they gave me with my picture, got me looking like a
stone-cold killer,
Ten-digit number, they say that I am an offender, there
must have been a mistake in the system,

Hook: Who ever thought that I would be like thi-s, locked
down in the state penitentiary,
I never thought that I would be like thi-s, locked down in
department of corrections,
Everyday it's the same thang, get up and ready for
inspection,
Everyday I'm anticipating, for a call out or a letter,
Who ever thought that I would be like thi-s, locked down in
the state penitentiary," he rapped.

"That was good lil bra. What they call you?" Triple J
asked.

"My name is Derrick Beasley, but everybody calls me
Lil DB," he replied.

"That was hard for real. You got talent," Triple J said
to him.

"Preshate that. I just rap about my life. All these other
rappers cap in they songs, but *This Shit the Realest.*

Chapter Five

*W*elcome to Frank D. Fairfield State Prison, Triple J read off the sign as they pulled onto the grounds of the most dangerous prison in all of Georgia. Ranked number one in prisoner deaths, Fairfield maintained its decade long reputation for extreme violence and officer corruption, even after the feds took over. No one wanted to visit Fairfield, not even the prison commissioner, without the national guard escorting him.

"How in the hell did I get sent here, with only five years?" Triple J questioned.

As the transfer bus pulled inside of the heavily secured gates, six giant sized CERT officers exited the intake doors. The prisoners aboard the bus watched as they marched information towards them, moving like a small military unit.

"Damn these crackers big asses fuck down here," one of the prisoners on the back of the bus said taking the words from everyone's mouth.

What he said was true, they were all huge. To keep a

little order, they had to be a force to maintain order amongst the states most vicious. As Triple J stared out of the window, he saw that the smallest CERT officer was around 6'6 320 pounds solid.

All these white boys look like they carry cows on their backs, Triple J thought.

"Gentleman, you all are going to step off the bus and stand on the black footprints," the transfer Sargent said over the speaker as the bus parked.

Fourteen prisoners on the bus and five of them came from diagnostics. The other nine have already been serving time and they looked like it.

The first man to step off the bus was a little fella of Hispanic descent. He didn't say a word during the transfer, but his heavy presence could be felt. His actual nationality was difficult to determine because his face was covered with prison tattoos. Triple J quickly labeled him as the short giant.

Next to exit were three black men. Overhearing their conversation on the bus, Triple J knew them to be of the same gang affiliation. They had a unique handshake with identical tattoos between their eyebrows; Triple J labeled them as the band of brothers. They all looked like they came from tough situations but one of them had it worse. He wore a long slash mark, raining down the right side of his face. Although it didn't look fresh, it looked like it caused him some pain because he kept his face screwed up on that side.

Damn they just sent me to some bullshit, Triple J thought as he stepped off the bus.

Mentally he was ready for whatever, strong in the mind.

"If your opponent can beat you mentally, he's already

won the fight," Triple J remembered his martial arts instructor telling him.

Off the bus and standing on the black footprints, the group of prisoners waited to be un-cuffed. Several minutes passed before two ranking officers, wearing white shirts, exited the intake doors with a tall black man wearing a suit. They all had very serious stares on their faces, like they'd been in the system for some time.

"My name is Deputy Warden Dupree, and I would like to welcome you gentleman to Fairfield State Prison. The stories you've heard are real and this prison is a very dangerous place. If you're here today, it's because you've fucked up at your last prison, pissed the wrong person off or my bosses, boss, boss felt you needed to be here. If you have a problem, it's not with me or my staff. We didn't send you here. Our only responsibility is to make sure you don't leave before you're supposed to. I'm not a babysitter I'm the Deputy Warden of Security. This is not a kiddie camp, so my best advice is to carry yourself as men and don't borrow shit. If you have an addiction, I pray you don't but pay your debts and you'll be alright," Deputy Warden Dupree said before walking off with the two white shirts.

Right as they were about to walk into the intake area a 1078 code was called over the radio. All six CERT officers took off running leaving the transfer officers alone with the new intakes.

"1078! That's a officer getting fucked up," one of the transferring prisoners said.

"Y'all grab your property and come on," the officer that drove the bus said.

As they walked inside, everyone was quiet. Triple J

didn't know how to mentally prepare himself for what was to come, so he got ready for whatever.

"You gone be alright. Just do ya time," he reminded himself.

For several minutes, heavy radio traffic could be heard over the officers' walkie-talkies before everything got completely silent. The transfer officers separated them into three groups before putting them in the holding cells.

The prison went on lockdown and for several hours, everyone sat in silence as they wondered what was going on. From the time the transfer officers left them until 8:45 pm, they saw no one. They weren't fed nor given anything to drink other than the water from the stainless-steel toilet sink.

A loud popping sound echoed down the hallway from the rear entrance. The night shift supervisor, Lt. Collier entered with a milk crate filled with plastic wrapped sand-wiches. Digging through his pocket he pulled out a set of several sets of keys looking through them before he found the one to their cells.

"Grab a pack out and leggo," he said referring to the sandwiches.

No one's property was searched and neither of them were stripped search or patted down. They didn't take intake photo's or see medical staff. Neither of them was angry about it; they all were actually glad to be out of those cells.

"Shit must've went up down here today," one of the black guys asked Lt. Collier.

He didn't reply, only shaking his head in disgust. All of the prison's staff were feeling it, after one of their own had been killed. Inmate.com had it that the rookie officer had tried to take a cell phone, but before he could get it, he was met with a machete sized makeshift knife in the chest. All of the staff were feeling his death, not just at Fairfield but around the state. They knew the job was hazardous, but not to the point one of them would be killed for doing their job.

All new arrivals were processed in G2, the intake dorm, before being classified for their permanent housing units. With 64 two-man cells, thirty-two on the top range and thirty-two on the bottom, the intake dorm housed up to 128 prisoners when filled. No one was ever locked down because the locks on the cell doors didn't work and officers didn't care.

In the sally-port entrance of G2 was brand new plastic bed mattress and clothing set-ups. The property officer had them prepared for the new intakes but after the prison went on lockdown they just moved to the sally port. Inside of the net bags were toiletries and uniforms, identical to the one Triple J received at prison diagnostics minus the orange uniforms. Inside were their state uniforms with the blue stripes.

"Y'all grab one of each," Lt. Collier said before he walked into the empty control. Waiting for them was a large crowd of men twenty or thirty plus while others watched from the top rails.

When Lt. Collier popped the door and they walked in they were greeted by the men.

"If you're coming from diagnostics, move to the right. If you came from another camp, move to my left," one of the prisoners said.

Several of them pulled out cell phones once everyone was separated. Individual pictures were taken and those affiliated with a prison gang were screened by someone from their organization. Those that weren't affiliated were labeled as civilians and had to hand over their discovery packets to be inspected.

Fairfield had a 100% death rate for snitches, and no one could hide their vetting process. It was quick and through, some even said state employees were involved.

After several minutes into the vetting, the nine prisoners that transferred from other prisons were cleared and assigned a cell. Triple J waited patiently with the others while they checked them out.

Concealing his true identity, he told everyone that he was a civilian. He felt that if their system was truly as good as they say, they would know who he truly was.

No lie, this shit really smooth, Triple J thought referring to the way they screened everyone coming in.

Three of the five guys from prison diagnostics were cleared leaving Triple J and Lil DB.

"You good?" Triple J asked Lil DB.

"Hell yeah! I'm on the case by myself. I ain't got no sucka shit on my name," he replied with aggression.

Upstairs in cell 212, was the compound boss, the man that oversaw the whole prison. Outside of his cell, were 24-hour security goons all lethal and ready to kill on command. It was very rare for the boss to exit his cell, other than to shower or an official call-out. Everyone in the dorm knew and was completely surprised when he did.

The room got quiet when his cell door opened, like a gust of wind had taken everyone's breath. Onlookers watched from their places as he and several of his goons marched down the stairs, all wearing menacing looks on their faces.

The crowd surrounding Lil DB and Triple J parted for them to enter watching as they walked straight to Triple J.

Staring down the ex-crime boss, Triple J showed no weakness as he stood face to face with the unknown man, looking him directly in the eyes. The man looked down at Triple J's hand and saw the scare.

"Do you know who I am?" He asked Triple J, mugging with a serious tone.

"Naw, but the real question is, do you know who I am?" Triple J replied, never blinking his eyes.

They both stared down each other, getting a feel for each other. Triple J didn't know what to make of the situation and wished he could get to the ice pick knife he hid in his lotion bottle. As they stared at each other, Triple J had no idea who dude was, but knew he had a lot of respect amongst the others.

He might have respect in here, but I got it around the world, Triple J thought as he analyzed the man.

The others around him mugged Triple J, but they weren't a major factor. If things went left, Triple J knew he had enough reach to grab their boss and hurt him severely. He knew he was outnumbered and also knew that if any harm was brought towards him, their entire last name would be annihilated within a twenty-four-hour time period.

Breaking the silence, the man began to speak.

"You know you look just like your daddy, but you got ya mama nose," he said.

Triple J had no idea who he was and wondered how he knew his family. He continued to stare but stood on the defense waiting on the man's next move.

"What's Up! Jone," the man said, holding out his arms for a hug.

A green light went off in his head and Triple J then knew exactly who he was. Growing up, he'd heard so much about his father's best friend Stacks. Although they'd never physically met but talked over the phone a lot while Triple J was young. Every time they talked Stacks always said the same thing, "What's Up, Jone."

Standing face to face with the man he'd known as his father's best friend, Triple J felt his time at Fairfield was going to be much smoother than originally expected.

This Shit the Realest.

Chapter Six

*M*eeting his dad's best friend in prison reminded Triple J of his old man's words.

"It's a treat when Playa's meet," Triple J remembered his father James Jay saying once after meeting a new business associate.

Serving a life sentence, Stacks had made a legendary name inside the state. Not only was he head of the Atlanta car, a group of guys from Atlanta that vowed to ride for each other inside, but he was also the compound boss. Everything that went on at Fairfield, was overseen by him.

"Thirty-three years of this shit nephew, it's time for me to get out now," he said to Triple J.

"I know of Unk. You've served your time," Triple J replied thinking how he'd been incarcerated one year longer than he'd been alive.

When Stacks got his life sentence, he only had to serve seven years before he was eligible for parole. Once he reached the seven-year mark, the pardons and parole board changed the time frame to fourteen years. Just as they did before, they moved the eligibility date to thirty years served before lifers were eligible for parole. It was a harsh thing but most lifers like Stack, did the time and never gave up on getting out.

"I know the streets are missing me," Stacks said as he reminisced about the streets of Atlanta with Triple J.

"The streets are definitely missing pieces, but I don't think they'll ever be found," Triple J replied.

"Da hell you talm bout man. Are you holding ya nuts on me?" Stacks asked with a chuckle.

"You have to think better of me than that, Unk," Triple J replied with a chuckle.

"Well, what you mean Jone?" Stacks asked again.

"The game has changed," Triple J began before Stack interrupted him.

"The game will never change, just the playas in it," Stacks said pointing at Triple J as he replied.

"And you're right. But if the new players don't play by the old rules. It's going to take more than you and me to fix it," Triple J replied to him.

"So, what you saying?" Stack asked.

"With all due respect. The streets ain't for men like you and me no more. We already did the streets now it's time to change it up and hit the executive suites," Triple J said.

"From the streets to the suites. I like that," Stacks replied, nodding his head up and down.

"That's right," Triple J replied.

"So, how exactly do you plan to do that?" Stacks asked.

"While I was in the county jail, we had to put an end to ANW. While I was there with the little homies, I saw how far I had actually grown from the crew and decided to fix it. We put an end to our illegal activities, and I set the guys up with legal business and started teaching them stock investing," Triple J said.

"Oh yeah?" Stacks asked, very interested in what Triple J was saying. "Y'all on some real next level, executive and CEO shit," he continued.

"It's funny you say that. Our new name is, The Executive Homies a Fraternity for black entrepreneur men," Triple J said.

"Okay then. So, you need to be called, The Executive Homeboy now," Stacks suggested with a chuckle.

"Yeah, that's what they me," Triple J replied, raising his hand as he chuckled with Stacks.

Stacks shook his head in agreement as Triple J talked. Seeing that his nephew was on the right track, Stacks stood from his bunk and grabbed a brand-new iPhone 14 from his wall locker.

"It's brand new. Never been used," he said, handing it to Triple J.

Triple J had been in the game selling phones and other illegal items in prison, so he knew the game.

"What you want for this?" He asked.

"I want you to get in touch with ya folks, it's yours," Stacks said, gifting his nephew with the iPhone.

Triple J had been in the game long enough to know nothing was free. In the streets the saying was, an even swap equals no swindling. Although stacks said it was a gift, he felt he was being swindled.

"I got the money, just tell me what you want," Triple J said.

"I told you it's a gift but since you insist, teach me how to trade stocks and invest legally and make me The Executive Uncle?" Stacks said, poking out his chest.

Triple J held the phone out like he was handing it back, to Stacks getting the surprised look on his face.

"We really do need an Executive Uncle," Triple J said with a chuckle before sealing the deal with an old fashion handshake.

Although they were excited to unite, Triple J was tired from the transfer. While they were talking, Stacks had the cell next to his cleared and cleaned for his nephew. He made sure neither of them had a bunkie and assigned two of his guys to stand guard outside of Triple J's cell.

"This place can get wicked. A lot of these young niggas got a lot of time they serving. They call it demon time and they ain't playing down here," he said to Triple J educating him on Fairfield.

Triple J was prepared for that. He had just left Rice Street a.k.a. Knife Street, doing time with the same young niggas Stacks spoke about.

They respect Unk, but like he said you could never be too cautious, Triple J thought.

Looking around his new cell, Triple J analyzed it just in case someone came inside, and he needed to defend himself. It didn't take long for him to scale the room, identifying several metal targets he would use to put someone's head through if an issue was to occur.

Once he got his cell organized to his liking, Triple J removed the iPhone Stacks had given him from his waistband. Remembering his iCloud login, he signed into his account and all of his old photos, contacts and emails were accessible.

The first number he dialed was his pops. When the old man didn't answer he began to worry knowing his father's health condition.

"Pick up the phone old man," he said to himself.

Thinking the number may just be foreign to him, Triple J texted their signature message.

"ET."

That meant to phone home, a message they adopted from the extraterrestrial movie E.T.

As he waited for Pop's to call back, he checked his emails before logging into the ANW Entertainment social media account. There were over 600 new direct messages and thousands of notifications.

When the page loaded, Triple J saw that he was tagged in several pictures of The Executive Homies. The most recent was a picture of his guys all wearing different color tracksuits with the red, white and blue Executive Homies emblem on top.

Triple J smiled to see that although he wasn't physically present, his homies had everything in motion. As he looked at the picture, Triple J remembered seeing the business proposal Flames had given him.

"We gone get rich off these clothes," Flames said.

Seeing the shirts *Same Hustle, Different Product,* Triple J smiled at their accomplishment.

This Shit the Realest.

Chapter Seven

*S*everal months had passed since Triple J arrived in Fairfield. Unlike his uncle, he refused to be cooped in his cell all day. Outside of the everyday hustling they put down, Triple J creates a daily routine for himself.

Every morning at 5 he removed the toothbrush from his door that kept it jammed shut. Like clockwork, one of the guys prepared a bottle of boiling hot water for him, so that he could drink his herbal tea. Although it wasn't scientifically proven Triple J felt the teas gave him natural energy and helped him trade stocks better.

Stacks had made money on the stock market following Triple J's teachings. One of the first things that Triple J taught him was to look at the current events before starting to trade, it gave market insight.

Yahoo finance was one of the reliable sources that Triple J trusted for financial news, and he checked the app throughout the day. There it showed financial news for companies on the stock market and government news that could sway the market. Once Triple J finished checking the news, he looked at several candle charts for companies he liked to trade on. Looking for different set-ups Triple J sent out different signals in The Executive Homies group chat. His years of market experience put the others at an advantage because it was very seldom that he sent out a bad signal.

"We all gone have private jets," one of his homies said.

From 6:30-7:45a.m that was his designated time to work out. Advancing from the normal push-ups and sit-ups routine, Triple J did HIIT, high intensity interval training, exercises punishing his body. Memorizing the workouts from different YouTube influencer's, he mimicked their workouts, seeing greater physical results over time. For the hour and fifteen-minute work-out he and one of his bodyguards banged out sets on the day room floor, while the other stood guard.

After reading an article in the Men's Health magazines, Triple J delegated fifteen minutes of his time to cool off before his 8am shower. Turning into a fitness junkie, the ex-crime boss, took cold showers post workout. An article he'd read stated cold showers were good for muscle recovery, so he took them.

The frigid temperatures had its effect on the muscles but, Triple J enjoyed the pick me up aftereffects of cold showers most. They were rejuvenating in energy, very much so needed in the depressing prison environment.

After the showers, he then got his days started. Stock trade and business consulting with The Executive Homies he stayed busy.

"What's up! Jone," Stacks said after he got dressed.

"What's up! Unk," Triple J replied after he came in.

Stacks was more excited than usual when he entered, like he'd recently received some exciting news.

"What you got going on Unk? Come in here showing off all your teeth. Have you got some go home papers?" Triple J asked with a chuckle.

"I ain't got no go home papers yet, but I got some nice to go home to," he said, bouncing his shoulders up and down with a huge smile.

"All this silly shit nigga, what you got going on?" Triple J asked with a laugh.

"Jone, I snatched me a fine lil tender last night. Twenty-three, light skinned, ruby red hair, hazel brown eyes, no stomach, fat ass and lil tits," Stacks said smiling from ear to ear.

Triple J could tell she had really excited the old man. Calculating the numbers in his head quickly, Triple J realized that he'd been incarcerated ten years longer than she'd been alive. Neither of them ever saw her in the flesh, but the way Stacks described her she had to be a real cutie, Triple J imagined.

"Where you catch her at?" Triple J asked.

"On the book. They got all kind of single, free world hoes on there. And guess what?" Stacks asked.

"What's that?"

"They love chain gang niggas," Stacks said very convincing.

For a lot of guys incarcerated, social media was their escape. Triple J ran the old ANW, revised The Executive Homies instapage, but never posted pictures of himself incarcerated. With his status quo, he knew the photos would go viral and that type of attention was the wrong attention for the ex-crime boss, especially since he was already down for a selfie, he'd taken incarcerated.

"You know a lot of them folks on there be fake Unk," Triple J said thinking she could be a catfish.

"You ain't telling me shit I don't already know, Jone. Krys ain't no catfish. We was on facetime all last night and this morning," Stacks replied with a full-face smile.

Although Stacks had been gone for a while he never missed a beat. He was very tech savvy and when he pulled out his iPhone and unlocked it with the facial recognition feature, Triple J laughed.

A picture of Krys was saved as his background photo like they'd been together for years.

When Triple J looked at the picture he smiled at his uncle.

"Okay then. I see you got ya some there," he said dapping up the OG.

"I told you, now it's time to get ya own, Jone," Stacks said before putting his phone back in his pocket.

Since the breakup with his wife, Jessica, Triple J had no plans of having a serious relationship again.

I'll never let another woman get close to me, he said to himself after the breakup.

"I know you think you're big shit but just think about it. You might find some on there you really like," Stacks said, trying to encourage him.

After giving it some thought Triple J finally agreed. Together he and his uncle created a new page for him and attached his dating profile. They uploaded a picture of him prior to incarceration and together they wrote his bio.

Hey Ladies, my name is James, and this is my first time trying a dating app. This is very nontraditional for me, but I'm putting forth my greatest effort in finding a match. I don't plan to be here long, but while I'm here let's vibe.

-The Executive Homeboy-

They continued setting up his profile and once he went live, Stacks left him to explore what was out there. Most of the women he saw were far from his type.

"Too much make-up, she looks like a man, I ain't feeling all this clowns weave she's wearing," he thought as he passed them up.

Right as he was about to give up, a beautiful brown skinned woman appeared on his screen. The face in her photo's looked familiar, but Triple J couldn't pinpoint if he knew her or not. He looked over her pictures some more before finally swiping right. He'd made contact and now all he had to do was wait for a response.

Stacks had got word that there wasn't going to be an inspection, so Triple J laid down, taking a trap nap. Just as he got good in his sleep his cell door opened, and he jumped up quickly.

"You good, Jone," Stacks said, realizing he'd startled him, when he entered. "Have you find ya some yet?" He asked.

"It's too many regular looking bitches on there. You know my ex-wife is the mayor's daughter, don't you?" Triple J asked.

"Young Jone got a going on," Stacks said as he shook his head.

Triple J was serious though. The only reason he gave the dating app a shot was because Stacks had convinced him. He had a fleet of real sexy career women with long money, begging for a shot with the ex-crime boss.

"I feel ya on all that, but check ya phone, Jone. See what's going on," Stacks said, more eager than him.

Triple J reached behind himself and dug the phone from his bed cuff. As soon as he unlocked the phone with his four-digit code, a match and message notification appeared. Triple J loosened up a bit knowing it had to be the pretty brown bunny responding.

Seated next to him, Stacks texted rapidly with his young joy, Krys. Triple J's new match Flayya had sent him a message he was not expecting.

"Hey Mr. James "Triple J" Johnson, Jr.

I wrote you a letter while you were at the Fulton Jail, but you never responded to me. I figured you wanted nothing to do with me and now it's ironic we match with each other on this dating app. I thought you were married and to my surprise you're on here. I had the baby and named him after you. He looks just like you and you're just in time for his second birthday. Call me," she said, leaving her number in the message.

Triple J handed Stacks the phone to read the message shaking his head.

"Look what you got me into," Triple J said.

After Stacks read the message, he smiled.

"Damn, nephew. You got women naming their kids after you?" Stacks asked.

"I think the child is mine," Triple J said.

"How you figure?" Stacks asked.

"When I got arrested in Texas, the Marshals flew me back to Atlanta on a commercial flight. This girl was the flight attendant, and she slid in the bathroom behind me while I was pissing. We had a quickie and bussed inside of her,"

"Swear?" Stacks asked with a smile on his face.

"Swear," Triple J replied. "When I was in the county, she wrote me and mentioned the baby, but you know how that go. I wanna see pictures of him first before I say he's mine," Triple J continued.

"Well, call her nephew," Stacks instructed him.

Triple J sent a text, and it was like she'd read his mind. Several photos of Baby James popped up on his screen and he knew immediately the boy was from him.

"Damn, this lil nigga look just like my baby pictures," Triple J said.

"Yeah, that's you, Jone," Stack replied, nodding his head.

Triple J smiled at the pictures of his little man and thought, *she could have lied about him being mines but, This Shit the Realest.*

Chapter Eight

Since finding out that he was a father, Triple J's life changed, and he felt better than ever. Parenting from prison had its difficulties, but since reuniting with his son's mom, it's been easier for him than most incarcerated fathers.

The unplanned pregnancy was a surprise to them both, but Ashleigh kept her job with the airline. Placed on light duty she worked in the corporate office, booking fights at customer service. While there, she was noticed by the higher ups, for her services and offered a less stressful position with higher pay as a liaison between airline and pilots union.

Accepting the gig during a pilot's strike, she worked diligently to calm things, all while being a full-time single mom. Earning just under seven figures a year, Ms. Flyya was a catch for every single man.

Although her job earnings were enough for her and Baby James, Triple J still transferred twenty-five hundred into her bank account every Friday. Fifteen hundred for his son and a stack for her.

"You know I don't need your money," she said to him once, not wanting to seem like a thirsty baby mama.

"I know! And you also know that Baby James is not your son alone," he replied.

When she got knocked up by The Triple J King of the A, she got knocked by a man that takes care of his responsibilities. Ten thousand a month wasn't a lot, but it was something coming from a man that she'd technically raped.

"So, what were you doing on a dating app? I know you don't have an issue getting a man," Triple J asked once during a casual conversation with Ashleigh.

"Most of the men in my career field are white. Before my grandma passed away, she told me to never be a white man's nigger bitch. So, I turn all of them down," she said.

"What about the black men?" He asked.

"The ones I've come across are either married or they have feminine ways. Like they're down low gay," she replied.

"So, what type of men are you attracted to?" Triple J asked genuinely wanting to know.

Ashleigh blushed for a second before replying.

"I'm into Corporate thugs," she said with a smile spreading across her face.

Triple J smiled with her, interested to know more.

"Interesting," he dragged out. "So, you like Corporate thugs. What's so attractive about them?" He asked.

"I love that dominating thug demeanor," she replied while being sexually charged by the conversation.

"I thought they call that a Alpha male. So, you're really attracted to Alpha men?" He asked.

"No!" She quickly replied. "I like Corporate thugs. I like hood niggas that can walk in the suites and close deals like they're still in the streets," she explained to him.

Triple J knew he fit the description perfectly of what she was describing. Her attractive energy was very strong towards him, and he liked it, but wanted to know more.

"I overstand," he said, pausing. "So, on the plane what was it that you saw in me?" He asked, always wondering.

"Well first let's be clear, I've never done that before. I don't even look at my passengers long enough to memorize their faces but when I saw you get out of that Tahoe my panties got messy," she said, letting out a soft breath. "Working for the airline, I've worked several prisoner transports, but yours was much different. The marshals flew you first class, you weren't wearing handcuffs, and they offered you alcohol. I knew that you were different, I just didn't know you was Triple J different," she continued.

Triple J didn't get the answer that he was looking for, but in so many words she let it be known that she respected him. The way she acted, he knew he had to be cautious with her because she could be ludicrous at times.

As she talked, he thought about what his dad once asked him.

"Which type of woman do you think is best for you son? A woman that you like or a woman that likes you?"

"The woman that I like," his adolescent mind answered.

Correcting him, his dad changed his perspective on dating.

"The best woman you can ever have is the woman that respects you," James Jay said. "Love leads to tears, but respect lasts for years," he reminded him.

Like so many others, Triple J knew she respected him and together they deleted their online dating profiles.

While things heated up with them, Stacks and Krys relationship had also strengthened. Using his administration connections, Stacks got both ladies and Baby James approved for visits without them sending in the significant other forms. Wasting no time, both ladies scheduled visits for the coming weekend, eager to see their men just as much as their men were.

On the day of visitation, Triple J called Ashleigh on face time as he got himself together.

"Hey Daddy," she said, answering on the first ring.

"What's Up Bae. How far are y'all now?" He asked ready to see them in person.

"Let me check," she said, pausing to look at her phone. "GPS says, we're thirty minutes away," she continued.

"True, I can't wait to see y'all," he continued smiling as he looked at his phone.

"Me 2," Ashleigh replied blushing at the camera. "Say hey to Daddy," she continued, turning the phone towards Baby James.

Seated in his seat like the prince that he was, a huge smile spread across his face.

"Baby James, Baby James," Triple J sang, smiling at his son.

Shying down in his seat, the little one tried to hide his handsome face.

"Stop doing, ya daddy like that," Ashleigh said, tickling his stomach as she drove.

Triple J noticed the silver designer emblem on her shirt when she turned towards their son.

Okay, Mama hitting these folks with the LV outfit, he thought.

"Alright! Keep ya eyes on the road. I'll see y'all when ya get here," Triple J said, seeing that she was distracted.

"Okay Daddy," she said.

"O-tay Da-de," Baby James replied, repeating after his mom.

They all laughed before ending the facetime call.

As he waited to be called out for visitation, excitement filled his heart. He was no mediocre dude, and Ashleigh was no mediocre chick. Although her father wasn't the mayor of Atlanta like his ex-wife, together they made a dynamic duo, Triple J thought.

"Say Jone, you ready?" Stacks asked, knocking at his cell.

"You already know Jone. Everything on like Pop Cone," Triple J replied, sounding like his dad.

Stacks laughed at the imitation. Not only did he sound like his dad, but he also looked just like him saying it.

"Like father, like son," Stacks said looking at his all grown up nephew.

Visitation began at 9:30am so to pass time, they kicked it in Triple J's cell, until they were called.

"Johnson and Hightower, y'all got visitation," the officer called over the intercom.

"Let's do it, Jone," Stack said as he stood from Triple J's bed.

"Let me hit some of that smell good," Triple J said before they walked out.

"Come on, Jone. You can't go wrong with the playa Cologne. This shit here reel the hoes on, like a com-a-long chain," Stacks replied feeling good as he bobbed and stepped.

"Alright, then," Triple J chuckled. "I need you to set a

playa like me straight, before I go on my visit date, to see my baby cakes," Triple J replied mimicking Stacks bobbing step.

Together they laughed as they entered Stacks cell. Immediately, recognizing the Sauvage bottle, same as he had at home, Triple J grabbed it and hit himself with a couple squirt on his shirt and neck.

"I ain't trying to be too loud," he said as he rubbed himself down.

Stacks laughed as he looked at his nephew.

Damn he's all grown up, he thought.

Together they walked to visitation, the first time Stacks had been outside the dormitory without his security goons. As they marched up the walk, guys from the other housing units watched them hard from their windows.

"I can't wait to see Lil Krys. She be talking all that shit on the phone about how she gone fuck the shit out of my old ass," Stacks said smiling ahead.

Triple J laughed, but his attention was on his surroundings. They were the compound bosses walking alone with no protection and everyone spotted that.

I should have brought my iron with me, he thought. *Naw we good, these niggas no better.*

As they walked into the backdoor of visitation, butterflies filled Triple J's stomach. The officer pat searched them both, before allowing them access to the visitation area.

One behind the other they entered, spotting Ashleigh and Krys, seated on the same side. Unable to hold back his tears, Triple J's eyes began to rain as soon as he saw his son.

This Shit the Realest.

Chapter Nine

$\mathcal{P}$rison had a way of changing those incarcerated. Some for the good, but most for the worst. As he stared down at his Uncle Stacks lifeless body, the only thing that filled his mind was vengeance.

Isolated in a holding cell, Triple J reflected on the day's events.

"This boy look just like your dad," Stacks said as he held Baby James.

Wearing matching outfits with his moms, Baby James walked back to his dad like a King. Triple J held his son and the love between the two could be immediately felt.

"What's up, Playa?" Triple J asked Baby James, holding his hand out for some dap.

"I not no playa," Baby James replied.

"What you mean you not no playa, son. You come from a blood line of playas. You're granddaddy a playa, you're daddy a playa, so that makes you a playa," Triple J said to him.

Baby James looked at his dad in disgust before he

pushed out of his arms. Running to his mom, Baby James climbed into her arms and looked at his dad.

"Mama, what's my name?" He asked.

"James," she replied.

"That's my name, Da-de not playa," he said, poking his chest out.

Although it was their first time physically meeting, Triple J knew this was his son. Baby James wasn't going for anything strange, and he demanded his respect.

"Re-spect, re-spect," Triple J replied, sounding like a Jamaican mon.

Turning his attention to his woman Triple J smiled at his child's mother. Although he and Ashleigh had a child together, it was their first time being together since his flight back to Atlanta.

"I know everyone compliment you on how well you look in your flight attendant's uniform, but today Ba-Bee you look a whole nother sexy," he said complimenting her in his ATL slang.

"What you trying to say I'm fat?" She asked jokingly with him.

"Naw, but that ass is," he shot back looking to the side of her chair.

Laughing out loud, she hit him on the hand.

"I wish you could slut me out right now," she said, biting down on her lip.

Looking around the room, Triple J looked for a place he could take her.

Damn, I wanna tear this pussy up real quick, he thought.

"Just relax," she said, touching his hand. "We gone set it up right for next time. We already got a airplane baby. Do you want a chain gang baby to? She asked.

Triple J smiled because how he was feeling, she could get a chain gang baby or a mop closet baby. It didn't matter; he just wanted to work towards making a baby.

As they were looking around, he was interrupted in thought.

"Ladies and gentlemen, we have fifteen minutes before visitation ends. We ask that you wrap up your visits and enjoy the rest of your day," the female officer said.

Triple J took advantage of the time they had remaining together. He and his son laughed and played together and right before they left, he and Ashleigh kissed for several seconds.

Damn I wanna tear this shit up, he thought as he grabbed her plush and round ass.

Baby James grabbed his dad's hand as they swapped spit and pulled it off his mom's butt.

"Ooh, check you out," Ashleigh said looking down at her son.

"No!" Baby James said checking his dad.

Little man wasn't going for none of that, they both realized. Krys and Stacks laughed at his innocent heart, finding joy in the protective moment.

Before departing Ashleigh placed a green and red bracelet on Triple J's left hand.

"Spirit told me to give this to you," she said. "It's to protect you from sudden death," she continued.

What in the hell do she got going on, he thought. *Spirit told me to give this to you.*

Triple J didn't understand what Ashleigh was into or what the bracelet meant, but he accepted it.

After being stripped and searched after visitation, Triple J and Stacks hit the walk together. As they approached E building, a gang of twelve plus exited and began walking towards them.

Triple J saw that the angry dozen was strapped up and ready for war. Stacks, being a prison vet, peeped the move and put his hand on his nephew's abdomen area, guiding him backwards.

"We gotta get out of here," Stacks said with a heavy gulp in his throat.

Outnumbered six to one, Triple J knew they didn't have a win and he and Stacks retreated as quickly as they could, getting back to the visiting area. As soon as Triple J entered, Stacks slammed the door, locking himself outside. Confused at what just happened, Triple J begins violently kicking the door from the inside, with hard front thrust kicks. Ample amounts of force were put into each kick, but it wasn't enough to breach maximum security lock.

Sargent White, the corrections officer that had just searched them, ran to the back at the sound of the kicks.

"Hey! Hey! Hey! What the fuck is you doing?" He yelled at Triple J.

"They're about to kill him," Triple J yelled back while still kicking the door.

As security his priority was to protect the remaining visitors inside. If an act of violence from the compound stemmed over into visitation, he knew his job and everyone else's on shift was over.

With all over his power, he rushed Triple J mid kick, tackling him to the floor. For several seconds they wrestled on the floor as the attack on Stacks took place on the other side.

"Let me go Sarge! Let me go!" Triple J yelled while being held on the floor.

"I can't do that," Sargent White screamed back. "I can't do that," he continued wrestling against the powerful Triple J.

On the other side of the door the commotion could be heard.

"Arhh," Stacks yelled in excruciating pain as he was being stabbed.

When the screams stopped, heavy tears began to pour from Triple J's face. All of the fight inside of him was gone as he and Sargent White together rained a small puddle of tears onto the floor.

This Shit the Realest.

Chapter Ten

*S*everal hours had passed, since Stacks life was taken and Triple J was feeling it. Inside of the holding tank he waited while the investigation took place. His body was still sweating as the heavy gulps of vengeance pumped through his veins.

I'm gone find you and I'm gone kill you, he said thinking about his uncle's killers. *Why didn't he just come inside with me? I should have let him go in first. Why did I survive?* His mind raced with thoughts.

Survivor's guilt began to set in flooding his brain.

"I should have died with him," he said aloud as the tears continued to flow from his eyes.

Usually on the weekend the CERT team was off, but after Stacks murder everyone was called in. Seated outside of Triple J's cell the ex-crime boss tried not to get too emotional, but losing his father's best friend had cut him way worse than the sharpest knife used to kill Stacks.

"Where were you?" Triple J imagined his father asking him.

I can't reply locked behind the door, he thought.

The backdoor of intake pooped, getting his attention. Standing from his chair, the CERT officer stood and greeted the three men that entered. He recognized one of them, the Warden of Security, but the other two he assumed were investigators based on their uniforms.

Tan cargo pants, black collared shirts with oval shaped gold badges, they gotta be GIB, he thought.

"How's he doing?" Triple J overheard one of them ask the CERT officer.

"It's affected him," the CERT officer replied.

"Okay, I'd like to have a word with him," one of the investigators said.

Triple J was placed in hand restraints, before the CERT officer opened the holding cell's door.

"Hey Mr. Johnson. My name is Special Investigator Ethan Thigpen. How are you doing today?" He asked.

"Don't get me to lying," Triple J responded, looking away from them.

"That's definitely not my intent. I'm actually here seeking the truth," he replied.

"Mr. Special Agent Sir, I appreciate you, but I'm not with answering questions. It's freezing in here and I just wanna go to my cell," Triple J said.

"I know exactly how you're feeling. I don't wanna be here neither. To be honest, I was actually at my son's baseball game when I got the call and I didn't get to see him at bat," he said looking at Triple J. "Just so you know, we have the maniacs involved on their way to Fairfield County Jail, where they will be charged in Mr. Hightower's murder. The only reason I'm here talking to you right now, is to make sure you also weren't involved," Special Agent Thigpen said.

Triple J looked at him in discuss. After such an insult, he thought about cursing the pig out, but refrained.

"What my partner was trying to say, we're concerned for your safety. If you don't tell us everything that you know, you could be next," the second investigator said.

Triple J immediately recognized they were trying to play him with the good cop, bad cop role. His conversation was very limited with law enforcement, especially investigators, and they had reached their limits.

"I would like to exercise my 5th amendment right and refuse to answer another question without counsel present," Triple J said, nodding his head.

"Alright then, you'll be going to county next," the smart mouth investigator said before they all walked out.

The cell door slammed behind them and Triple J knew they didn't give a damn about him. The feelings were mutual; he just wanted to get along.

When the CERT officer returned and removed the handcuffs, Triple J's mind went crazy.

I'm about to turn this bih up, he thought as they walked back to his dormitory.

Stacks murder put the entire state on immediate lockdown per the commissioner. All of the sally-port gates were secured with a chain and lock, Triple J saw when he returned.

At the door several of Stack's most loyal soldiers stood ready for war.

"He can't come in here," one of them said.

"Chill, before you hurt yourself," Triple J heard G Code tell him.

Since Stacks was gone, G Code was the next man inline for the compound. He'd been incarcerated eighteen years and survived several prison wars, riding for the Atlanta car. Although the others felt like Triple J left Stacks hanging, G Code knew different.

"I need to holla at you," G Code said to Triple J when he walked in.

"I need to holla at all of y'all," Triple J said pointing towards his cell.

Walking in without security was different, but he didn't need them. He'd always been able to take care of himself and the only reason he'd ever used them was because of Stacks.

When he opened his cell door, he realized his cell had been destroyed.

"The GIB Investigators came and went through both of y'all cells," G Code said when Triple J looked confused. "They boxed up a lot of y'all shit, but I grabbed this before they came," he continued pulling Triple J's phone from his pocket.

Triple J looked at him in suspense, wondering if the GIB investigators had really been there.

"How did you know where to find my phone?" Triple J asked.

"I been surviving for so long in this shit. I checked where I hide my horn, in the dirty clothes bag," he said.

"Why should I trust you?" Triple J asked.

"Shawty, they don't call me G Code for nothing," he responded.

Triple J had the gift of discernment and for several seconds he stared into G Codes eyes, looking for a sign of dishonesty. When he felt the man could be trusted he opened up.

"It wasn't supposed to happen like that," Triple J stated, beating himself on the head.

"What wasn't suppose to happen like that?" G Code asked.

"Before we walked into visitation, I felt something wasn't right. The niggas in E building watched us walk all the way to Viso, but never said shit. Unk wasn't paying attention, he was so caught up on seeing shawty that he missed the whole play," Triple J told G Code.

"Missed what play?" G Code asked.

"That they was mounting up. We suppose to died together. We suppose to died together," Triple J said as tears began to fall from his face again.

"Listen to me Shawty, you gotta tell me everything. I got us we just gotta move different," G Code said.

Triple J gave his version of what happened and when he finished, G Code knew it to be true. One of the mules had already relayed Sargent White's version and both stories matched.

"Listen Shawty, Dolla kept us separated for whatever reason. I don't know why, but he's dead now. When we first started doing time Dolla use to call himself Stacks. Something happened and twelve put him on Administrative Segregation. Rumor was somebody had put a million-dollar bounty on his head for something related to his case, but you know how inmate.com goes. The crazy thing was, he only let you call him Stacks. He made everybody here call him Dolla, even me and I know Jone from the streets. I know you wanna get some answers, so let me get my ear to the streets and I'm gone keep you updated," G Code said before stepping out of Triple J's cell.

A heavy wave of confusion had hit him, leaving Triple J lost at sea. He promised himself that when he found out who was behind the million-dollar hit, mayhem was due.

This Shit the Realest.

Chapter Eleven

*F*or several days, Triple J dreaded making the call to his father, but he knew that he had to. As the phone rang his heart rate picked up and there was a long pause once his father answered.

"Hello son. Are you there?" James Jay asked.

"Yes, I'm here," Triple J responded after a heavy sigh.

"What's going on Junior?" He asked, calling him by his juvenile moniker.

"Jone gone," he said, voice filled with pain.

James Jay had love for his lifelong friend but loved his son more. After Triple J finished telling his version of the story he kicked into Pastor Johnson mode.

"Let us pray," he paused. "Most Merciful, Most Magnificent, Lord God, Leader and Teacher, we come to you today, giving all praise for the blessings that you rain down over our lives. We thank you, for the life that you give and the lives you've call home to sit with you. Lord God, right now we thank you, for my brother Stacks life and we thank you for the stain that he's left on this world. We pray to you right now, Lord God, asking that you give strength to all of his friends and loved ones affected by this sudden tragedy. We know that nothing is ordained without your permission, so we leave vengeance to you," James Jay prayed.

At that point Triple J didn't want to hear any more.

Vengeance is mines, he thought.

When his father finished crying out to the heavens, he cried out to his son.

"This battle is not yours, it's the Lords," he said, reminding his son.

"For you maybe, but for me this is personal," Triple J replied.

Knowing the real truth, James Jay struggled not to tell his son what happened. He knew that trying to convince Triple J to change his uncompromising mind would be more difficult than sneaking the devil into heaven.

"Alright son. Take care of yourself," James Jay said, allowing him to make his own decision before ending the call.

The warmth in his father's voice could be felt through the phone. As he thought about the relationship he shared with his father, he thought about his own son.

"Fatherhood over every hood," he said to himself.

So much had changed in his life leaving him in an emotional wreck. Triple J knew that he had to think rationally because one bad decision could be the cause of his demise.

Self-preservation is the first preservation, he reminded himself.

As he planned his next move, he knew to avoid the heat, he had to get out of prison. Right after he pulled out his phone to call his attorney, his phone began to vibrate.

"Hello," he answered.

"My Brother," the male voice replied.

Immediately, Triple J recognized the voice of his good buddy.

"The Don," Triple J sung.

Outside of his family, DonJuan was the one of the few he trusted.

"You're coming home," DonJuan said.

Like the timing couldn't be more perfect, Triple J smiled at the wonderful news.

"How soon?" He asked.

"Very," DonJuan replied.

Since his first day of incarceration, the only thing he wished for was to get out. Hearing the news from DonJuan was like an upbeat musical tune.

"I appreciate that," Triple J said before ending the call.

Triple J knew that if anybody knew the truth it would be DonJuan. He had access to Triple J's great uncle, the Godfather and he would know.

Next, he called his attorney Torris J. When he didn't answer his personal phone Triple J called the office.

"Thank you for calling the law office of Torris J. Esquire. How may I direct your call," a female voice answered.

"Hey Samantha, this is James," Triple J said, recognizing the woman's voice.

"Oh, Hey Triple J. How's it going?" She asked.

"Fair to midline, I couldn't ask for more," he replied in his business voice.

"Oh great," she replied.

Samantha was Torris's wife and law partner. She was also an attorney with law licenses in several states, but never presented cases, letting her husband have all of the shine. In the Atlanta Legal Tribune, a special article was written about her, headline reading, "Is She the Next, or the Hidden Best?"

Triple J being a friend of the Johannes family he knew the truth; she just let him do what he did.

They both were great attorneys and since Triple J's conviction, his appeal was their focus. His high-profile appeal was a must have because it would keep them in the rankings for America's Top Attorney Award, presented by the American Bar Association. Everyone loved awards, even attorneys.

"Torris is on a call right now, but if you give me one second, I can get him off for you," Samantha continued.

"Thank you," he replied.

As he waited for Torris to join the call, his mind went back to his Uncle Stacks.

Damn, Unk supposed to be on the turf with me, he thought.

Torris picked up the call in Torris's office and a white male's voice could be heard speaking on another phone.

"Yes, Torris. The paperwork has been faxed to the sheriff's office. Right now, we're just waiting for them to contact the DOC to arrange his pickup. Mr. Johnson should be back in Atlanta tomorrow morning. I'll get Judge Oliver to sign off on his appeal bond today and he'll be processed out as soon as he gets to Fulton Jail," ADA Earl Sullivan said.

"Alright, keep me updated if anything changes," TJ replied ending the call.

Loud screams could be heard next as Triple J listened.

"Yes! Yes! Yes!" TJ screamed. "I told you I was going to get you the fuck out of there," he continued.

Triple J was thankful, excited and depressed all at the same time. His time had come, and he was ready to get back to his life.

"You heard what the ADA said. Now, I need you to stay out of the way. The sheriff's office will be there to pick you up within the next twenty-four hours," TJ continued.

Triple J didn't ask questions ending the call with a smile on his face. The text alert from DonJuan vibrated his phone and immediately he saw the news link pertaining to his case.

News Alert

"Atlanta's most notorious crime boss has slipped through the cracks of the justice system yet once again. Yesterday a private session was held in Appeals court regarding the case of James Johnson, Jr. versus the State.

Some of you may remember Mr. Johnson, who goes by the moniker Triple J, from a story that we covered two and a half years ago where state's RICO charges against him and twenty-seven of his Ape's & Wolves crime family associate were dismissed. Those charges ranged from street corner hustling to the murder of Clearance "Little C" Coleman.

He and his lawyers were able to wiggle free on the severe charges, but retired Superior court Judge Ben O'Hare showed no remorse to Mr. Triple J at sentencing for a jailhouse cell phone a photo of him was found in. The ex-crime boss was given the maximum sentence of five years to serve in the Department of Corrections with no jail credit given.

At this time, we have no details of the appeal, but my sources say a DOJ investigation has been launched against several state agencies following the ruling. My name is Melissa Waters, and this is Atlanta's Number one news source WISN.

This Shit the Realest.

Chapter Twelve

*O*utside of the Fulton Jail, several news vans lined the driveway to the main entrance. The whole U.S. waited and watched to see the release of the ATL notorious crime boss and businessman.

As a safety precaution, Sheriff Ahmad Christian, assigned members of his personal protection detail to escort the Atlanta crime boss vehicles away from the jail's property.

"Are you ready," Torris J asked his client.

"This shit is wild," Triple J replied, reflecting over his time inside. "I almost died in this jail and now I'm on my way out," he continued, truly thankful inside.

It had been several years since he wore regular clothes. Before the release, Ashleigh met with one of Triple J's associates, delivering him one of The Executive Homies navy blue tracksuits. His attorney wore his custom Tag Heuer watch and took it off his wrist, gifting it to the ex-crime boss. James Jay couldn't let his son exit looking less than a boss, so he removed his gold trimmed Cazal eyeglasses and handed them to him.

Triple J rolled his shoulders back and lifted his head, locking his eyes ahead. His attorneys led him out to the podium, with Ashleigh on his side. Several deputies stood to the side, keeping the paparazzi and reporters at a safe distance.

"Two years ago, my client told me that he was innocent, and I told him that I would do everything in my power to prove it. I gave my word and today I can say, I kept it. Despite the heavyweights we've been up against, this appeal is just the surface of what's to come. Mr. Johnson has had a very tough time away and would like to quietly spend time with his family. Out of respect for you all here today we're going to limit the questions to three," TJ said before stepping back.

Several news reporters began to yell questions at the podium.

"Mr. Johnson, since you've been away, major crimes in Atlanta have decreased 18%. Now that you've returned should the community be worried about your ANW crime family," one reporter asked.

"I'm a businessman and I have nothing to do with major crimes in Atlanta. I actually wore this sweater today to introduce The Executive Homies Fraternity. We're an Atlanta based collection of male entrepreneurs that mentor trouble and at-risk youth. We provide them with the tools and years of experience we have, guiding them to become businessmen and entrepreneurs," Triple J replied.

Several people in the crowd clapped as the questions continued to roll in.

"So now that you're out, will we see you and Mayor Reeves' daughter together again," another reporter asked.

"A lot has changed since I've been away. I'll always love the mayor's family, but now that I'm home, I'm focused on a new way of life with new adventures," Triple J replied, looking back at Ashleigh.

Her eyes told and all, she was in love with the man at the podium.

"Your attorney said you've had a rough time. Was he referring to the murder you're being investigated for at Fairfield?" The last reporter asked.

Triple J froze at the podium as he was reminded of the horrific day.

"Thank you. That's all we have for you today," his attorney said interrupting.

Triple J wanted to walk away, but his feet wouldn't move. Staring at the reporter for a few more seconds he began to speak.

"Stacks was my father's best friend and brother. When the DOC transferred me to the worst prison in the state, he sacrificed himself to make sure that I lived," Triple J paused and placed his right hand over his heart as tears filled his eyes. "I ask that y'all remember my Uncle Stacks as one of the most honorable and respected men to ever walk this earth," he continued before walking away from the podium.

A black bulletproof Cadillac waited with the rear door ajar at the jail's curve. Triple J and Ashleigh climbed into the back and the caravan pulled away with camera's following them away.

"You did a good job today," Ashleigh said, rubbing her hands on the back of his neck. "I know you loved Stacks," she continued looking at him with her beautiful brown eyes.

Ashleigh pre-arranged for the sitter to watch Baby James for two nights, while she welcomed his dad home. Wasting no time, she raised the window blocking the driver's view inside of their executive ride. The vehicle was spacious enough for her to fall onto her knees in front of him. Not saying a word, she loosened the drawstring to his joggers and pulled his limped baby maker out.

Using both hands, Ashleigh massaged his man while kissing the tip.

"You already with the shit's," Triple J said while slightly raising from the seat pulling his pants down.

"You looked stressed daddy and it's my job to make sure you're not," she continued while still kissing his mans.

When Ashleigh slid her warm and wet mouth down his shaft, Triple J exhaled heavily from the sensitive signal racing through his body.

While incarcerated, Triple J kept his mans in his hands, but that was no comparison to Ashleigh's oral extravaganza. Too much for him he ejected in seconds releasing a heavy load of semen into her mouth.

Ashleigh looked at him and smiled as she swallowed their unborn children.

"Are you good now?" She asked.

Triple J smiled at her before laying his back on the white cushioned chair.

This Shit the Realest.

Chapter Thirteen

$\mathcal{T}$he first week out of prison was much different than he planned. Several local and some national news networks repeatedly showed his release, creating popularity for the ex-crime boss.

He and Ashleigh planned to relax and spend time with the family, but after several of his old business associates contacted him, he was back to being Triple J the businessman. While meeting with The Executive Homeboy, several of them delivered large amounts of cash. Some of them were gifts while others were old debts being settled, now that he was home. Triple J found it funny that so many forgot about him while he was incarcerated but patronized him when he returned.

I guess the saying is true, when you're out of sight, you're out of mind, he thought.

While away, several small-time hustlers tried to fill his shoes but didn't know the knock to get certain doors opened. Triple J heard about them while away but instead of leaving them lost, he invited them to join him and The Executive Homies.

Joining our fraternity gives you access to Atlanta's elite," he said.

And that it did, they quickly learned.

"There's this building on downtown Mitchell Street that has been vacant for years. The previous owners lost it during litigations and the banks are just holding it. I reached, but no one has responded," Omar "Big O" Knight said.

Twenty-six-year-old, Omar stood 6 '7 and weighed 328 pounds. He was built like an action figure, and his depth made him appear larger. Several years younger than Triple J, he carried himself like he was an OG, earning the moniker Big O.

Omar was very business savvy, but white businessmen were intimidated by his large stature and facial tattoo markings. Stereotyped as a gang banging thug, even though he'd never done anything illegal, they refused to take him seriously, up until The Executive Homeboy stepped in.

"It's been a while since I contacted my old banker friend. No promises, but I think I can get you a call back," Triple J said after looking over the building plans he drew up.

The plans were impressive, Triple J thought. Omar was going to turn the old Mitchell Street building into a high-rise community. The lower levels would be shopping centers, while the upper floors were condominiums.

Triple J knew that The Executive Homies needed a downtown headquarters. Helping Omar get the property, would give him the wanted address down where they needed to be.

Like Big O, several other visitors met with him, regarding their business issues. He was the power company to the plugs and after all of his meetings, $$$, was all that flashed in his head.

Once a hustler, always a hustler. One thing about me I'm gone get me some money, if I don't do nothing else, he thought.

Seven days after being released, Triple J counted over a million dollars in his cash stash. No one knew where he kept his money on his home property, but they knew he was back on the grind.

Before his release, Ashleigh heard about the 75-acre ranch that one of the airline executives planned to put on the market. With her salary alone, she couldn't afford it. With Triple J's pockets all things were possible.

Just 45 minutes outside of Atlanta, the Hampton property was a true definition of heaven on earth. It had its own private lake for fishing, tennis and basketball courts and several other amenities across the property. Because he was still legally married to his ex-Jessica, they purchased the property in their son's name, adding it directly to his trust.

That one purchase had Baby James listed as the youngest documented millionaire in the state, with a net worth of 7.6 million U.S. dollars.

"This lil nigga already rich as shit," Triple J said jokingly after their closing.

It was everything he wanted, to leave an inheritance to his offspring. The goal was to leave them so much that his grandchildren's children would be able to live off his wealth.

Everything in his life was going well, but he still struggled knowing the killers behind his Uncle Stacks murder were still alive. He wanted to let things work out in the universe but deep down he couldn't let it go unanswered.

While G Code was working his move on the inside, Triple J hired help on the outside to check as well.

Several of his old hitters, from the ANW Hunters crew, had started a security company while he was inside. They called themselves The Executive's Force Protective Services. They did everything from club events to celebrity escorts throughout Atlanta and surrounding southeast states. While the others were satisfied with being guards, three of them took advantage of the legitimized company and obtained licenses to do private investigations.

They were licensed goons, with all of the high-tech spy gear, gadgets and equipment.

When Triple J got alone with them, he handed over all of the documents that he had on the case.

"This is personal to me," he said in a serious tone.

"Understood," they replied, respecting their old boss.

This Shit the Realest.

Chapter Fourteen

*B*eing a family man was something the ex-crime boss enjoyed, especially waking to his beautiful fiancé every morning.

"You are so fucking handsome I just want to scream," Ashleigh said waking Triple J with his herbal tea.

Stretching his arms, he sat up on his California King size bed.

"Thank you love," he said before kissing his lady, Angel.

Ashleigh had become the joy to his life, capturing him constantly with her high vibration energy. Every time Triple J thought about her, a smile erupted across his face, making the ex-crime boss blush.

"I love you," she said, kissing him with her beautiful bubble lips.

Growing up in the urban community, both Ashleigh and Triple J witnessed a lot growing up. They were both raised in single father households and while Ashleigh's father struggled to keep her away from the pimps and corner boys, James Jay was teaching his son how to break a bitch and flip a nick.

They both had a lot in common, but culturally things were different. James Jay taught his son from the Bible, while Ashleigh's father taught her the ways of Yoruba culture.

Living in Atlanta, Triple J heard conversations about Ifá but was never interested. His focus was on getting to the money that religion rarely crossed his mind. With Ashleigh being a Yoruba priestess, he was open to learn about her and her cultural ways.

"So many people confuse Ifá for a religion but it's not. Ifá has religion in it but it's not a religion," she said first as she explained the culture to him.

As she explained Ifá to him, he processed what she was saying and a lot of it made sense. Especially, paying homage to the ancestors.

Once she was finished giving him the basics of Ifá, Triple J told her about his comatose experience with the ancestors.

"I never told you this, but before I woke from the coma, I met my ancestors. My great-great-grandfather and so many more. There were these African spear warriors that saved me from the water, and I even hugged my mom," he said remembering what he could.

As he told her the story, Ashleigh remembered her experience with the Egun while in priesthood.

Triple J sipped his morning tea from the bed edge while Ashleigh sat next to him. She loved being in his presence, especially during their downtime.

"We have all of this land daddy, I think we should start a farm," she said to him, starting a conversation.

Growing up in the City of Atlanta, he dreamed of one day having a farm. He knew he would have to hire cowboys because there was no way he would be the one milking cows or raising chickens every day.

When she mentioned the farm, it was a déjà vu moment for him.

"I'm gone be the man that tells everybody else what to do," young James said as a kid.

Triple J thought for a second before responding.

"Having a farm takes a lot of responsibility and it's very time consuming. Right now, I don't have that to give love. If it's something that you want to do, I'll support you as best as I can, but I'm out," he said, trying to show his lady some support.

"I understand," she said with sadness in her voice.

"Please, don't do that. You know I have a lot going on," he said.

"Well, I came to you because I don't want this to be a me thing. I know how you love The Executive Homies, and I was thinking we should use the farm to educate the young men y'all mentor," she said, getting his attention. "You don't have to do the work. We can hire someone to teach the teens how to raise their own animals and grow their own food. With you being the business genius that you are, you can teach them business stuff, like ordering animal feed, purchasing fencing material and the buy and sell of farm animals. We can turn this into a whole program for the youth teaching them how to live off the land," she continued.

Mentioning The Executive Homies, was enough to get his undivided attention. As Ashleigh spoke, he thought of all the ways they could monetize the farm. Breeding and selling farm animals were cool, but not enough.

As he thought, he remembered reading about the property tax breaks farmers have. With livestock on their land, he would be able to live damn near free, avoiding the government thugs. Also, with a legitimate nonprofit organization operating on the property they qualified for income tax breaks and other benefits.

"The federal government has all of these grants for farming. If we set up a program within The Executive Homies, that would make us eligible for all kinds of federal and educational funding," he said. "I'm gonna talk to my friend, Professor Hughes, at the State University and see how we can offer paid internships. This idea may be great after all, just give me a little time to research," he said as he began to calculate their next move.

"I love it. I think this could be something we set up for Baby James's property to make money in the family forever," she said.

Triple J smiled and kissed Ashleigh for her great idea.

As soon as she walked away, he sent out a message to his colleagues in The Executive Homies group chat for their opinions.

"We're thinking about starting a school for farming on the property. It's going to be a project for The Executive Homies. What's y'all thoughts?" He asked.

As soon as he sent the message a text from G Code hit his phone.

"Call me, ASAP!" The text read.

Triple J assumed the message had something to do with his Uncle Stacks death and called quickly. When G Code answered he didn't know what to expect.

"The light skinned nigga they call Crazy Ahk, do you remember him?" G Code asked.

"Yeah, the strip head," Triple J replied.

"Yeah! These niggas were about to bury the boy, but held up because he mentioned you," G-Code said.

"What he got to do with me. That nigga from the Mac not my side of the track," Triple J replied.

"Yeah, I know. He name dropping though. Say y'all supposed to be some kin," G-Code said.

"Hell naw," Triple J said quickly.

"He says he's ya brother or ya girl brother, I don't know, I just wanted to check before they finish him," G Code continued.

Triple J knew he was no kin to him and doubted if he was to Ashleigh because she never mentioned a brother.

"You know he don't have enough P to be related to me, but I'll ask her," he replied.

Triple J didn't care for outsiders and definitely didn't care for a junkie. Crazy Ahk was a stripper, one that smoked an unknown chemical off small strips of paper and nodded like a heroin addict. He tried to be cool, but lame was his middle name.

Triple J walked into the bathroom, while Ashleigh was doing her make-up. For a few seconds he stared at her before asking the question.

"You never told me you had a brother," he said looking for her reaction.

Ashleigh turned towards him with a surprised look on her face.

"Tunde," she said, calling out his name.

Triple J looked at her and knew then that it was about to get crazy.

This Shit the Realest.

Chapter Fifteen

*W*hile incarcerated, Triple J learned that prison was a place full of surprises. There it was a who's who and everybody swore they had a going on before they got knocked.

Triple J wasn't really social with the guys inside but witnessed a lot. One day while the incentive meals were being passed out, he witnessed a father and son met for the first time.

"That's your daddy," Stacks said to him.

"I don't know this nigga," Lil Westside replied in a stern tone. "He been locked up my whole life. The streets is the only daddy I know," he continued.

Lil Westside's words were harsh but also the honest truth. For many black children in America, the male absences were their reality leaving the streets to raise the young soul.

To verify that Crazy Ahk was her brother, Triple J requested a picture of him. The picture was so gruesome that he didn't want to show her.

Damn, they beat the kufi off that nigga head, Triple J thought as he stared as his swollen peanut head.

His hands were tied to the bed rails, and his face was beaten badly, almost unrecognizable.

Years had passed since Ashleigh last saw her brother and it was a little difficult to see him. She continued to stare at the picture until she recognized his distinctive facial birthmark. Immediately, tears began to pour from her face falling onto the phone's surface.

"What happened to him?" She asked genuinely concerned.

"He owes money and didn't pay," Triple J replied.

"How much I'll send it now," she said, grabbing her phone as the tears began to flow heavily.

Ashleigh's hands shook rapidly as she tried to unlock her phone. Triple J quickly grabbed her, laying her head on his chest before she had a panic attack.

"Calm down, I got this," he said, squeezing her in his arms.

Calming her in his arms, tears slowed, and she stopped shaking as much.

"Cut him loose and clean him up," Triple J said, instructing G Code when he answered.

"Aite," he replied, and the call ended.

Triple J knew his reputation was one of much respect and not to be reckoned with. Whatever debt Crazy Ahk owed, now belonged to him and it was much more than what he originally owed for using his name.

While they waited for the call back, Ashleigh began to tell him the story of how they were separated.

"When our mother died in the car crash, the government took us because my Baba didn't have a place for us to go. Me and Tunde were separated and when Baba got things right, Tunde had already been adopted and taken some place far away. Baba told me one day, that Tunde will return and we will have a big and pretty house for him to come," she said.

Triple J heard her, but he didn't care much for a Junkie. After selling drugs for so long all an addict could get from him was out his face.

When G Code called back, Triple J and Ashleigh sat on the recliner sofa before answering the Facetime call.

"You tryna holla at buddy," G Code asked.

Triple J looked over at Ashleigh before he answered.

"Yeah, let me holla at him," he replied.

When Crazy Ahk got the phone, Triple J stared at him in disgust.

"You know you some bull shit," Triple J spat at him.

Ashleigh seated on the side of him, squeezed his hand reminding him that Crazy Ahk was her brother.

"I know big bra, I know. I swear to you I ain't on no bull shit, I was doing right," he said.

"How? You got them folks shit and didn't pay what you owe em," Triple J said.

"Two months ago, my adopted mom died from Covid. She would send me money every other week, but when she died the money stopped and I ain't have nobody else to call. I asked Allah for help and that's when I saw a woman getting in that nice truck after visitation. She looked like my sister, but I didn't know. I tried to holla at you after visitation, but OG Dolla had got killed and I knew you had a lot to deal with," he said.

"I heard all that, I'm talking about them folks and they money,"

"I tried. I promise I tried to work the money off, but they kept putting interest on me. They act like they my slave master or some shit with all the bullshit. I tried to pay off my tab, but they think I'm gone keep being a slave," he said standing up for himself.

Triple J understood what he was saying, but there was a cost for going into debt.

"So, while ya mama sending you money for food and shit, you get high and about to get killed because you're an addict?" Triple J asked.

"I know. I know," he said, sounding just like all the other junkies Triple J knew.

"Since you know everything, you know you owe me now, right?" Triple J asked.

"I know big bra. I know," he continued.

"Well check this, ya sister is my woman not a drug sponsor. She's not sending you no money or paying off your debts. I'm gone dead that situation and you know I'm gone have them niggas watching you. If you smoke anything else, I'm gone leave you to dry out after they wet you up," Triple J said.

Crazy Ahk knew he was serious and didn't want to test the waters. Nobody was safe at Fairfield, but he knew with Triple J dating his sister, there was a chance for a better life.

Triple J said what he needed to say before handing Ashleigh the phone. He knew she wanted to catch up with her brother and gave them a chance, walking out the room. As they spoke, he felt the love between them. Although he didn't care for junkies, he was glad that she reconnected with her brother seeing the dream come true.

This Shit the Realest.

Chapter Sixteen

*a*fter finding out about her brother, Triple J realized there was a lot about Ashleigh that he didn't know. He felt that he learned a lot about her, during their incarcerated calls, but it was only what she wanted him to know.

Contacting the nanny, Triple J made overnight preparations for Baby James, while he planned a night to remember with Ashleigh.

Premier's Restaurant & Bar was the one place you could meet anyone from State Senators to Fortune 500 Companies Ceos. Very popular amongst the ATL elite, their earliest table reservations were six months away.

Contacting one of his old friends, the owner of Premier's, Triple J did what no one else has ever done, making same day reservations for two. Being the powerful man that he was, Triple J was gifted with top tier service as a welcome home gift.

"Yeah man, this one is special," Triple J said to his buddy, referring to Ashleigh.

"Don't worry about anything James, we got ya," he replied.

Once everything was set, Triple J made the text.

Triple J: Be Ready at 8

Ashleigh: What's the occasion?

It was all a surprise and kept it that way.

Triple J: Check ya Zelle.

Ashleigh had no idea what he had up his sleeve. Once she checked her account and saw the 5-thousand-dollar Zelle transfer, she instantly put on a smile.

"I'm going shopping. I'm going shopping," she said, dancing down the hallway to their bedroom.

At exactly 7:58 pm, two Cadillac Executive SUVs pulled down their driveway. Parked at their front door, eight men dressed in black suits exited and filed around their trucks posting up like the secret service. Opening the back door, Triple J exited walking alone to the front door of his home ringing the doorbell.

Marisa, their nanny, opened the front door and smiled at the well-dressed Triple J.

"Why didn't you use your key," Ashleigh said from their upstairs room.

"Good evening, Ma'am, my name is James and I'm here to take your daughter out tonight," he said roll playing.

"I'm sorry Mr. James. Ashleigh's not my daughter, but I'll run and fetch her for you sir," Ms. Marisa said, going along with Triple J.

"Madam Ashleigh. Your guest is here," Triple J could hear Ms. Marisa say from the top of their stairs.

Ashleigh had no idea what was going on and was in total shock when she saw him standing well-dressed at the bottom of their staircase.

Dressed in a white tuxedo with black scrambled stitching on the lapel, Triple J stood with a dozen red roses in his hand. He was well dressed for the occasion, but Ashleigh's dress had him mesmerized. He watched her throw her hips as she swayed her curvaceous hips down each step.

"May I?" Triple J asked, reaching for her hand at the last step.

Ashleigh grabbed his hand and smiled at his kind gesture.

Keeping it P, he handed her the flowers and extended his right arm to escort her out of the door. Tears of joy began to fall from her beautiful eyes as they walked to the idling SUV's.

"You good?" Triple J asked, genuinely concerned.

"I've never had anyone ever do anything like this for me," she said.

"Well, you deserve it," Triple J replied as they climbed into the truck.

Ashleigh was his son's mother, and she was a damn good one. When she wasn't working at the airline office, her time was spent taking care of her home and her two men inside.

With lightly played Hip & B music in the background, he gave her the corporate thug experience she yearned so much for. As they were chauffeured through the city, the two of them held hands vibing in conversation.

"I love you for this," Ashleigh said, staring deep into his eyes.

"Damn, lil baby. This the only reason you love me?" He asked, looking at her with surprise on his face.

"No silly," she said, slapping him on the arm. "You're

just so different and you make me feel amazing," she continued.

"As you should," he said, kissing the top of her hand.

Ashleigh enjoyed the lifestyle that came with Triple J, but she had no idea what he had planned next.

As the two SUV's pulled into Premier's parking lot a large crowd could be seen. Waldo, the restaurant's owner, arranged for Triple J and his date to receive the elite red-carpet treatment, giving them all the bells and whistles.

Seated behind the curtains, Ashleigh had no idea what waited for them on the outside. Triple J's security team gathered on the right side of the vehicle, creating a barrier around the truck from the paparazzi photographers. Once Triple J tapped on the window, the backdoor was opened, and rapid camera flashes captured every step of the returning King and his Queen as they stepped out.

In total shock, Ashleigh got caught with a smile on her face spreading from ear to ear.

"I'm gone tell the world about you just so they can get jealous," the lyrics to future song played as he kissed her on the red carpet.

This Shit the Realest.

Chapter Seventeen

*F*or many ATLiens, living the rich and famous lifestyle was the one dream they always wanted. For Triple J it was his reality, every time he left the house. Greeted by the restaurant's owner and his wife, Triple J and Ashleigh were personally escorted to their seats by the bosses.

"When we heard that you were coming tonight, Waldo canceled our fight to France, so that we can be here to meet the new Mrs. Johnson," Patrizia Simone, Waldo's wife, said to Ashleigh. "You have an amazing husband and I'm so glad to see that he's back," she continued.

Patrizia and her husband loved Triple J, especially after he bailed them out during their tough financial times.

"He is. And I'm so thankful to have him home," Ashleigh replied, squeezing Triple J's arm as they walked.

"You are one lucky woman to have my friend James. You make sure you take care of him," Waldo said, feeding into the conversation.

"Oh Waldo, I'm in great hands. Ashleigh's the impressive one. She doesn't like attention, but I have to tell you. She's the brains that ended the 3-month airline strike at Hartsville. This woman is brilliant and to be honest, I'm the lucky guy to have her," Triple J said redirecting all of the attention to his woman.

"Impressive, thank God she's on our side James," he said, raising his hands to the roof. "If my employees ever go on a strike, I know who to call," Waldo joked, causing the room to erupt in laughter. "Well, the two of you enjoy dinner and I'll swing by later to check on you," Waldo continued.

As soon as the owners stepped away the celebration began. Two glasses were sitting in front of them and the server poured them half full glasses of champagne. It had been a while since the ex-crime boss had drunk alcohol, but he still sipped. He didn't want to drink much, staying focused on the objective at hand.

I gotta get her to open up to me tonight, he reminded himself.

Waldo pre-arranged for them to have the best experience while at his restaurant. They were assigned the most beautiful waitress in the town capturing the eyes of both Triple J and Ashleigh.

Philippine and Black, Anastasia captivated everyone she crossed. Standing 5 '8 with long and pretty black hair, her body was perfectly proportionate, with a well-rounded asset hanging off the bottom of her back.

As a flight attendant, Ashleigh was used to seeing beautiful women from all over the world, but Anastasia was different. Her sex appeal was so magnetic, she attracted both men and women.

After the amazing meal and a few glasses of champaign, Ashleigh had loosened up. The question she popped after dinner, surprised both Triple J and the server.

"As you know, my fiancé was recently released, and this is his celebration dinner. I looked all over the menu, and I didn't see it, but I know he would love you for dessert," she said. What's it going to take for you to leave with us tonight?" She asked.

Triple J watched Ashleigh's body language and saw that she was familiar with the female experience.

"Well, I have my shift," Anastasia said before being interrupted.

"Don't worry about that, it's already covered," Ashleigh said, robbing her of an excuse.

They all knew the owners were fans of Triple J and their server girl wouldn't be missed if they took her away early that night. After taking pictures with the owner's and goodbyes were exchanged the couple departed Premiere's with her.

The security team made a spin around the block to pick up Anastasia's car. Because they were going to an undisclosed location, they grabbed her cell phone and car keys, assigning one of the agents to trail the caravan.

The Castle was Triple J's downtown Penthouse, not many knew about. It wasn't his biggest property, but it was where he went when he wanted to overlook Atlanta. It was usually rented on his Day Rentals website, but the reservation was canceled for them to close out their evening there.

Ashleigh had never been there but walked in like it was their home. She stepped out of her heels at the door and dropped her designer dress to the floor right beside them.

"Last one to shower is a rotten egg," she said, running through the penthouse nude.

Triple J watched as her big ole ass bounced while she ran through the living area.

"Girl you is silly," he said as he watched.

Anastasia following lead also got undressed and ran behind her new best friend.

The word beautiful was an understatement to describe Anastasia because she was a life size Goddess. Colorful tattoo ink ran across her body, giving her the appearance of a magazine model after the photoshop edits.

Triple J smiled as he undressed thinking to himself, *Tonight is going to be one that we all remember.*

From the bathroom entrance, he could see both Ashleigh and Anastasia's silhouette connected on the other side of the fogged glass. Both ladies were locked at the lips and their hands held on another. Triple J looked in the mirror at himself and thought, *This Shit the Realest.*

Chapter Eighteen

$\mathcal{T}$he next morning, Triple J left the two of them asleep in bed, while he went out to run morning errands. Usually, Ashleigh would get up before him, but the previous night's extravaganza had her tranquilized.

Damn, that lil shit was wild last night, he thought as he went to meet with his partner.

Triple J had money invested all over Atlanta, from commercial real estate to luxury car rentals. Since being released he'd been out of sight, staying at his Hampton home.

"So, what makes you wanna start a farm?" his brother The Executive Flames asked.

"To be honest, it was Bae's idea. She mentioned it a couple mornings ago and at first, I wasn't really feeling it. She said we should do it for The Executive Homies, another way to save the youth," Triple J said.

"I feel you; I just don't understand how that saves our youth," Flamez said.

"We had all kinds of dreams to become professional

baseball players, basketball players and football players because that's who we saw with the big houses and money on TV. In the hood, we seen all the dope boys living out the dream, with nice whips, big rims and diamond chains. They had all the fine girls in the apartments, the ones we liked as kids.

We've already learned what the dope boy dream gets us, a Rico indictment. So, if we show them a different life better than standing on the corner, we've given the boys a better option to choose from," Triple J said.

"I feel you, but that farm shit is a lot," Flames said.

"Maybe for us, but not them," Triple J replied quickly.

What Flamez was saying, farming was a lot for an adult whose mind was already fixed on what they wanted. Triple J agreed part of that to be true, but not for the youth. Most adults in America ran from labor work, but the youth were excited to learn new things, especially with animals. Allowing them to see the farm's financial reports, once everything got started, Triple J believed it would show them how hard work pays off in the end.

After meeting Flames, Triple J made a few stops before heading back to The Castle.

Thinking about the two, Triple J checked the cameras from his phone. He saw that they were awake and actively enjoying themselves. Ashleigh had her head between Anastasia's legs, manipulating the waitress's vagina with her super wet mouth.

From the camera angle, Ashleigh's ass was up and facing the bedroom door.

"I'm bout to beat that the shit out of that pussy," he said to himself as he rode up the elevator.

Creeping into the front door, Triple J went straight to the bedroom and drew down on the two.

"Oh shit," Ashleigh jerked, surprised that he was back.

Triple J slid inside of her slow stroking as her pussy opened up.

"Y'all like having fun without me?" he asked, grabbing her by the ass, diving deep inside.

"I'm so-orry," she said in between strokes.

Triple J sexed her like it was his first day out, long stroking her pussy like he still lived in the projects.

"Them ghetto goods," he called it.

Ashleigh was no slouch, gripping his mans in between her vagina walls as he punished her pussy.

"You about to make me cum," Ashleigh screamed as he continued.

Her body began to quiver, as Triple J continued the pounding. He didn't let up on sexing her, like they were trying to make their second child.

"Ooh shit, I'm cummin Daddy! I'm cummin!" She screamed before falling to the bed.

"Bring yo ass the fuck over here," he said aggressive to Anastasia.

She had been fingering herself while they were getting it in. She crawled towards him headfirst, and he immediately put his healthy erection in her mouth.

Slurping on his rod Anastasia sucked it like she had something to prove.

Triple J held her face up from under the chin and stroked her mouth in a circular motion.

"Open wide!" He said, slapping her jaw with his free hand. "I wanna feel the back of your throat."

Anastasia struggled to take all of his rod in her mouth, gagging on the thick tip.

"You love this dick?" He asked her with his rod still in her mouth.

Anastasia tried to answer, but her mouth was filled. She looked up at Triple J and shook her head signaling yes.

"Come get some then," he said.

Tatted all over her body, Anastasia had a big colorful butterfly tattooed in her ass. Triple J guided her around rubbing her ass as she turned it towards him. Bending at the back, she laid her face onto the bed creating a beautiful arch, spreading the butterfly wide.

Triple J wasted no time sliding into her vagina walls. Like a plumber he laid the pipe filling her walls with his well girth god given torch.

"Oh my..." She said losing her voice. "It fe-eels so good," she continued to say eyes rolling into the back of her head.

"I know girl. Take it," Ashleigh said standing behind Triple J, pushing his back forward.

Hands down, his sex game was too much for one woman. Ashleigh kissed him in the mouth, spreading out his focus so that Anastasia didn't get punished so much.

"Get on ya knees," he said to Ashleigh as he continued pumping inside of Anastasia.

He pulled out his mans and ejected his heavy load inside of Ashleigh's mouth. Anastasia refusing to be left out began, turned around and began kissing her new best friend, exchanging Triple J's semen in their mouths.

This Shit the Realest.

Chapter Nineteen

*I*ncarceration in America, had a hidden way of destroying the lives of its incarcerated men, especially those returning to society. Despite how hard they worked to transition, most struggled with untreated mental disorders that affected their everyday lives.

On the outside, Triple J appeared to be fine, those close to him saw that he was damaged. Struggling with PTSD, loud popping sounds triggered the ex-prisoner, putting him on go mode.

"Are you okay?" Ashleigh asked, noticing a murderous stare in his eyes, after she closed the bathroom cabinet.

"Yeah, I'm good. Why you ask me that?" He asked with aggression.

"You just looked different," she replied.

Triple J felt normal, but over time Ashleigh noticed that his behaviors began to worsen. She became uncomfortable around him alone and that was unhealthy for their relationship.

One evening, while their son was playing with his

plastic bat, Triple J snapped and scared them all. The noise freaked him, and he grabbed his gun before running outside. When he didn't see anyone, he began letting off shots shooting towards the tree line.

"Come on, mother fuckers. Come on," he said in between gun blasts. "Y'all killed my uncle, and I promise you I ain't going out like that," he continued to shoot his AR-15.

Baby James screamed, while his dad was shooting, dropping his bat as he frantically ran to his mother. Neither of the two had any idea of what to do other than stay down and out of his way.

Ashleigh was in desperate need of help, but she couldn't call the police for it. Triple J was out on an appeals bond and having firearms in his possession would violate the stipulations and possibly send him back to prison.

"Daddy please stop shooting," Ashleigh called out to him. "I checked the cameras. There's no one out there," she said, trying to bring him back.

"Go back inside. I know what I heard," he continued to yell.

"It was the baby," she spat back at him with tears flowing from her eyes. "He was playing with the bat. I heard it too," she said as she cried.

Triple J looked down at the yellow plastic bat on the ground where his son was playing. He saw his son held by his mother as they kneeled at the garage door crying. Triple J scanned around the house again before he laid his gun onto the ground.

"I'm so sorry," he said, walking to them and holding them in his arms. "Y'all all I got, and I refuse to let anything happen to you," he said, kissing them both on the top of their heads.

"I know daddy. I know," Ashleigh replied before kissing him back.

The next day she arranged for him to see a mental health professional that specializes in treatment for ex-cons. Initially, he refused to see a shrink, until he heard her optimum.

"It's either you go to therapy or we're leaving," she said.

Possibly losing his family, Triple J agreed under one condition. The therapist had to sign a nondisclosure agreement.

Ashleigh got the therapist to sign in front of Triple J, promising that no one outside of the three of them could ever know about his treatments. Triple J knew he had a lot bottled up and needed serious help. During his first therapy session, he opened up to the therapist participating in the treatment activities.

"Thank you for agreeing to this session Mr. Johnson. I know it must be hard for you to talk to a stranger," the therapist began. "Is there anything bothering you right now that you care to talk about?" The therapist asked.

Triple J looked at him for a second before he looked down at the floor.

"While I was in prison, my dad's best friend was killed and every day I hear his screams in my head and the sounds of them stabbing him," Triple J said before his eyes exploded into tears.

As Triple J cried the therapist took notes on his white legal pad, before handing him a tissue paper to dry his eyes.

"I can't say that I know how you feel because I don't. What I do know is the first stage of the healing process is letting go. We as men tend to bottle our feelings, holding the pain inside. You crying right now is a great sign for me because it lets me know you really want to heal from this trauma," he said softly while touching Triple J's shoulder. "On my way over here, I was prepared to confront this hard core, strong headed guy that's done prison time and feels like the world is against him. I'm in total shock right now because for someone as strong headed as you are, opening up so suddenly signifies to me that you're ready to heal. And that's all I'm here for my brother," he said with a smile erupting on his face.

His calm and healing energy brought peace into Triple J's life and that was what he needed most. While they talked, Ashleigh listened from afar. She was so thankful that they had a good first session and couldn't wait to see how his progress came.

"Thank you for agreeing," she said to him.

"No, thank you for not leaving. You're my heartbeat and if you take that away I'm left with nothing," he said to her.

Ashleigh smiled and hugged her man tight within her arms.

This Shit the Realest.

Chapter Twenty

*L*oving is caring, just as harmony is to peace. Outside of his close friends and family, not many saw the ex-crime boss after his release.

The weekly meetings with his therapist had helped his healing process and Triple J implemented the therapy recommendations into his life.

"I know your time in prison was traumatic, but you're no longer there. As a free man, you shouldn't have to suffer because you survived. For starters, I want you to visit places you've felt most comfortable in the past," he said.

It didn't take long for him to realize that he was most comfortable in his old Grant Park neighborhood. There, everyone loved him. From the old ladies that ran the community, to the little kids he bought toys for every Christmas. It had been years since he saw everyone, so he put together a plan. Sending out the message in The Executive Homies group chat, he let everyone know that he was going to throw a Welcome Home/Block Party for the King.

Making the park reservations, a newbie in the park and

reservations department tried to deny him access to the park but using his political connections, he was able to get it done. At the councilman's request, Triple J agreed to hire off duty police officers to manage and maintain order throughout the park on the day he reserved, along with his private security.

They expected for everyone and their Mama's to attend, especially the ghetto Section 8 girl.

"Bih, that nigga gone have all his rich friends out there. I know I'm gone fuck me a baller today," he imagined them saying.

The block party wasn't just for him, but also The Executive Homies. Triple J hired Greg, one of his Executive Homies that had a barbeque restaurant to cater the event. They estimated 10 thousand attendees, so that was going to be a lot of food.

"This shit is going to be big; can you handle it?" He asked Greg.

"The real question is can it handle me?" Greg asked, shooting back.

Triple J directly contacted several of the vendors that he wanted to use and got things arranged. Ashleigh wanted to be the event coordinator when she heard what he was doing, but he wouldn't let her.

"You're standing next to me," he said, hugging her in his arms. "Remember why this is even happening. I'm supposed to surround myself with the people I feel most comfortable around. There's no one closer to me, than the woman I sleep next to every night," Triple J said, pecking her lips as they rocked back and forth in each other's arms.

"Well, can Anastasia, do it? She's good at hosting events," Ashleigh suggested.

Triple J looked at her and smiled.

"You like her for real. Don't ya?" Triple J asked.

Ashleigh couldn't hold back her feelings for the beautiful woman, blushing at the question.

"That's Bae, but I love you more Daddy," she said, pecking his lips three times.

Triple J stared at her as he thought. He and his ex-wife Jessica shared a woman in the past, but never the same woman twice. Anastasia was a baddie, and her sex game was on point.

Although she was a server at his friend's restaurant, he didn't know how she would do directing the hood event.

This is a different crowd. A whole lot of rowdy mother fuckers, he thought before answering Ashleigh.

"You know how important this is to me. You're asking me to fuck with her in my old neighborhood where shit gets real. Them project girls will cut her just because she's prettier than them," Triple J said.

"Stop tripping, everything will be fine," Ashleigh said with a chuckle. "They know this is your event and if she's working for you, nobody will ever touch her," she continued.

Ashleigh was right. No one would touch her in his hood, especially knowing she was connected to him. After several seconds of thinking he finally replied.

"Alright, call her up," he said.

Ashleigh removed her phone from her back pocket and dialed Anastasia's number. When she didn't answer she sent a text.

Ashleigh: Tap in, Bae.

Laying in his arms, Triple J saw the message she sent and laughed at her lesbian love side.

This is going to be interesting, he thought about the three of them.

Polygamy had become popular in the black community, attracting couples to a third and fourth partner.

While he held her, Ashleigh melted in his arms.

"I love you, Daddy," she said, emotionally attached to him.

So many thoughts ran through his mind as laid there, Triple J began to really wonder. Sexing different women was fun before, but now that he was building a legacy he was on a different time.

If Anastasia was going to be around, he needed to find out how she would fit into everything. Before he could ask, Ashleigh had already given him her answer.

"If she does a good job with the block party, I want her to be our girl. We can have a poly relationship. Me, You and our girl against the world," she said, throwing up her three fingers like it was a gang sign.

Triple J never imagined himself being in a polygamy relationship, but as he thought about it, he smiled.

This Shit the Realest.

Chapter Twenty-One

On the day of the block party, Triple J arranged for close homies, to meet with him at the ranch. He and Flamez surprised them with a leather motorcycle style vest, stitched with The Executive Homie patch on the back.

"When we ride, we ride together," Triple J said to them all.

Since starting the clothing line, Flamez has done well, traveling across the country, promoting The Executive Homies brand.

"We're getting more love with The Executive Homies than we did with the Apes and Wolves," Flamez said once to Triple J. "Everybody fucking with our campaign."

On the website, he sold everything from hats to slides, with The Executive Homies logo on them. People paid for anything and everything that The Executive Homies logo was on, even the pencils and pens. Although they loved the tracksuits his best sellers were the slogan t-shirts.

Power in the Pen not the Pistol, Boardrooms over Bricks, and the most famous *Same Hustle, Different Product.*

Everybody loved the movement, even the OGs before him.

"Ken-Tay told me to tell ya, he sees what you're doing in the streets. Showing these young niggas a better way," his cousin Issac said to him.

Issac was well known in the streets, representing the famous Jonesboro South projects. After two prison bids, Issac was able to find his wave, starting his own production company.

While everyone in Atlanta chose to rap, he found his niche in artist management. Two of his artists, Prince Slick and Jr-Boy 4 were able to close major distribution deals and while they were spending up their money, Issac invested.

"Cuz, I got the cranes for the camera's, production lights and trailers for the actors' make-up and shit. Everything they need on set, we got it even," he said to Triple J trying to impress him with his success.

No one outside of Ashleigh and his therapist knew the real reason he decided to throw the block party. As he conversed with his cousin, he wondered if he struggled with a post-prison mental disorder.

"You're not by yourself," he remembered his therapist saying. "There are so many guys like you that go untreated."

As he looked around at all of his homies, he wondered if any of them struggled like he did.

We all in this shit together, he said to himself in thought. *Now this is what family looks like,* he continued.

Everyone loaded into their cars and trucks and together they pulled off the property with a security escort. As they rode, the flashing blue lights on the escort vehicles reminded him of the times he went to court.

Triple J grabbed Ashleigh's hand to remind himself that he was free and no longer handcuffed or shackled.

"We're in the back of the Double R," he said to her smiling.

Ashleigh didn't know what he was thinking but squeezed his hand and kissed him. She held her man's hand tight, showing the love and comfort that he desperately needed.

As Triple J looked at her, he thought, *My definition of a rider.*

Downtown they got off at the Boulevard exit. Triple J smiled as he rode through his old neighborhood remembering his youth years.

"Ms. Dot use to stay right there. She had the best Icey cups when we were growing up," Triple J told Ashleigh.

They caravan pulled up to the park Triple J could see the long line of cars parked along the streets.

"You mention my name and bring the whole city out," he said to Ashleigh, instantly excited.

Everybody loves The Executive Homeboy. He was one of the pillars in the community that kept the hoods together from afar.

Stringed together over the park's driveway, were red, white and blue balloons spelling, Welcome Home Triple J. So many people had lined the side of the driveway, greeting The Executive Homies caravan with smiles and waves as they arrived.

The police had the parking lot roped off for them and their cars to park near the park's gymnasium.

Outside of Triple J's ride, so many people piled around with their phones pointed at the car. Ashleigh squeezed

Triple J's hand as the security team created distance around the car.

"Are you ready?" She asked him.

"Yeah, Let's do it," Triple J said to her before signaling the security with a single knock on the window.

This Shit the Realest

Chapter Twenty-Two

*T*wo days after the welcome home block party, Ashleigh invited her bestie boo, Anastasia, over to the ranch for dinner. At Triple J's request for pasta, their chef prepared his favorite spaghetti and meatballs dish with garlic bread and salad as the side.

The trio waited on the back deck, as their food was being prepared, reminiscing over the successful welcome home event.

"When I first started planning the block party, Ashleigh insisted that you handle things," Triple J said leading the conversation. "To be honest, I didn't know what to expect. I wondered what kind of taste you would bring to the hood and how the people would receive you," he paused. "You amazed me and the rest of my homies with the thought and detail you put into everything. The love could be felt through the community because of you," he said complimenting her.

"So, I wasn't wrong by asking you to let her organize things?" Ashleigh asked like she didn't already know.

"No, you weren't. I loved everything the day brought, especially you," Triple J replied, squeezing Ashleigh's hand as he stared into her eyes.

"Aww, thank you," Anastasia replied blushing at the two. "I think the people loved it the most," she continued.

It was true, Anastasia did an amazing job, and all of The Executive Homies loved her. After the event, several of Triple J's Executive Homies contacted him wanting her to coordinate their next event.

During the planning process, Anastasia had full access to all of his executive contacts and emails. Using an email blast, she invited all of them to be a part of his official welcome home party.

Lil B, his good friend that worked as a radio host, was first to email her back, with his producers on board to air the welcome home party live on the radio.

"When they get wind of this, the whole city coming out," Lil B said to them full of excitement.

The radio producers showed up with their staging equipment and street team to engage with the crowd.

When Sylvester Oliver, CEO of Atlanta's number one record label CQ, heard about the event, he canceled his artist out of town shows.

"They've got to be at Triple J release party. This is going to be bigger than Birthday Bash," he said to his team.

Several of Triple J's famous friends hit her back wanting to participate in the festivities. Since they had access to the gymnasium, Anastasia organized a Celebrity Basketball fundraiser.

"All monetary contributions are going towards the construction for The Executive Homies Farming Academy," she said to them.

Surprisingly, they raised over 150k, more than enough to start the construction.

The entire day was beautiful and filled with joy. Issac's production staff showed up with their equipment recording and photographed the event, capturing very memorable moments.

Before departing, Triple J gave an executive speech and thanked everyone for their support and contributions, leaving the town in style.

"I'm just glad I was a part of your special day," Anastasia said as they reminisce over the party.

As they sat on the back deck, Baby James ran outside playing with his ball.

"Catch," he said, throwing it at his daddy.

As soon as he released the ball, he flew along with it, falling flat to his stomach. He'd fell hard knocking the wind out of his little body and it scared him buckeyes. Anastasia didn't have kids, but she quickly jumped into mommy mode, helping the frightened crying child.

"It's okay! You're okay," she said, bouncing him in her arms.

Tears ran down his face, as he laid his head on her shoulder. Triple J and Ashleigh surrounded him, comforting their baby boy as he cried.

"That was a good throw, but you've gotta slow down, son," Triple J said when he got right.

Ashleigh tried grabbing him, but he pulled away staying with Anastasia.

"Oh, you like her?" Ashleigh asked.

"Yes!" He replied, "She's my mommy number two," he continued.

Ashleigh looked at Triple J and smiled. It was their plan

to ask Anastasia to join their relationship after dinner, but that time was perfect.

"Hey Anastasia," Ashleigh said, getting her attention. "Baby James says you're his Mommie number two. How do you feel about actually being his Mommie number two?" She asked, pulling out an engagement ring.

Anastasia was blindsided with the surprise looking back and forth from Ashleigh to Triple J.

"Are y'all serious?" She asked with a jaw dropping look on her face.

"Please?" Baby James sung like he was in on the surprise.

Anastasia began to cry, and Baby James made everyone smile.

"It's o-tay Mom-e. Don't cry. It's gone be o-tay," he said to her, wiping her eyes.

Anastasia began to shake her head up and down, lost for words.

"Yes! Yes! Yes!" She screamed with a huge smile stretched across her face.

She sat Baby James down and held out her hand. Both Ashleigh and Triple J slid the ring on her hand together, locking in their trio.

The three of them hugged, making a triangle with Baby James standing in the center. Triple J looked at them both and said, "Now, This Shit the Realest."

Chapter Twenty-Three

*T*riple J knew his life would get better, post incarceration, but to what level he didn't know. He never imagined in a million years that he'd be engaged to two women at the same time.

I can get use to this poly lifestyle, Triple J thought.

Both Ashleigh and Anastasia wanted to become Johnson's. Before doing so, Triple J went and talked to his dad.

"I know you saw me with different women when you were growing up, but that was stressful son," his father James Jay said to him.

The kidney cancer had taken a hold on the OG, putting him in the cancer treatment center. Every week, Triple J visited the hospital, spending hours with his old man. He didn't like his dad being there, but James Jay loved it. Especially the young pretty nurses.

"This is my heaven on earth," he said to Triple J once referring to how well they treated him.

When Triple J told him about the engagement with Ashleigh and Anastasia the old man was opposed.

"I know, Pop, but this is different," Triple J said to his dad. "Neither of your women liked the other and they always fought. My fiancés brought to me is a lot different from your situation. They work together, cook together and we all live together. They call each other sisters and we're enjoying life together," Triple J explained to his dad.

"So how am I supposed to marry y'all son?" James Jay asked going into pastor mode.

"They're planning a trip to Africa, so that we can have a Yoruba wedding. That's what they want and over there it will be no discrepancy marrying them both," Triple J replied.

"Yoruba? Son, I don't know about no Yoruba or Aruba. I know Hallelujah. I know the father, the son and the Holy Spirit. You were born in America and raised in America. I ain't from Africa, so I don't know how the African people do things, but over here you marry one woman. That mess you got going on must be something from ya mama side," James Jay replied, snapping on his son.

Triple J laughed at his father's correct response. He'd spoken to a Priest in Africa and during the call he told Triple J the ancestors on his mother's side were the ones protecting him.

"Just admit it pops. I'm the best that's ever done it," Triple J replied with a smile.

James Jay couldn't knock his son; he was always unpredictable. Since a child, Triple J had been successful at some amazing things. When he handed over the family, he didn't think his son would elevate as high, nor as quick as he did in the game. Hands down, Pop Johnson had to admit that his son was the best to ever do it.

"You're a hard block," he said to his son, referring to him as a rock.

"I'm just a chip off the block," he shot back laughing with his dad.

They enjoyed every moment together. Especially, when reminiscing over life.

"I remember when you were three and you had that red and yellow big wheel. You had the lil girls pushing you up the hill and when you rode down, they chased behind you. I knew then that you were different," James Jay said to his son.

"Some things are just in ya and not on ya," Triple J replied with a smile.

Although they enjoyed each other's company, the real issue was still there. James Jay had fallen very weak from kidney cancer, and it was taken a hold of him. Still kicking it with his smooth and cool attitude, everyday he struggled.

"Some days are cool and other days I be ready to go. Truth is, I just wanted to see my boy come home," his father said before closing his eyes.

"I'm home now pops. Ain't no going back," he continued.

"Now it's time for me to go home," he said with a single tear rolling down his face.

Triple J held his father's hand from the edge of his hospital bed.

"I got us," Triple J said as the tears rained from his face.

Grieving in silence, Triple J sat with his father's lifeless body, until the hospital's visitation hours were up.

"Mr. Johnson, we're sorry about your loss, but that's your time sir," the medical nurse said when she entered the room.

Triple J held his father's hand as he stood up.

"I got us," he repeated before slowly departing.

As he walked to his car, he continued to mourn in silence. The skies were dark and cloudy like a rainstorm was on the way. The sun had found one spot to sneak through landing on top of the hospital. Triple J followed the light into the skies, and it appeared to be a portal to heaven.

Immediately, his tears stopped, and a smile stretched across his face.

"You're home now," he said with a smile. "You're home now."

This Shit the Realest.

Chapter Twenty-Four

*T*he streets of Atlanta were filled with heavy traffic, as the funeral procession, for James Johnson Sr, drove to the church. Hazard lights flashed for miles with members of The Executive Homies new and old crew paying their respect.

"Your father was my good friend," Pierre the Mafia Godfathers from Detroit said to him. "I owed your old man a favor that's still valid. So, if you ever need me, I'm one call away," he continued.

Triple J knew his father was loved and respected by crime families all over the county. When he became a pastor, many of them called him to oversee their religious ceremonies and services.

As they pulled up to the church, Triple J's heart rate increased. Ashleigh felt the energy shift through his hand and offered comfort.

"There is no reason to be sad, Daddy. He's in a great place," she reminded him of the results they were given after performing an ancestral ceremony for him.

Triple J looked at her and smiled, but deep down he was hurting inside. His father was his best friend and the one person he knew to have his absolute best interest. With James Jay gone he didn't know who to trust wholeheartedly.

"Ifá guides," Ashleigh said, reminding him as they stopped in front of the church.

The funeral was open to the public but for safety purposes, the entire Executive Force security staff were on hand, along with off-duty Sheriff deputies. Those in attendance were screened for weapons and explosive devices, before entering the church and only a few people were allowed cell phones inside.

With security escorting them Triple J, Baby James, Ashleigh and Anastasia were quickly ushered inside.

"The first family is entering the building," one of them said into his lapel mic.

They were escorted downstairs to the pastor's chambers, while everyone else in the caravan was screened by security. Once all clear was given, Triple J and his family were escorted into the church from the back stairs.

As they entered, Triple J saw there was a packed house. The first row was reserved for him and his family, but before they went to their seats, they stopped by the custom 24k gold casket.

They made you look good, Triple J thought as he looked down at his father with a smile.

Wearing a white tailor-made tuxedo jacket with gold scramble eggs on the lapel, James Jay was literally casket fresh. Triple J recognized his father's body was relaxed and a slight smile was on his face.

Baby James looked from his father's arms staring down at the old man.

"Is Papa going to wake up?" He asked.

"Papa is awake. He's living in the afterlife," Triple J said to his son.

"Will I be able to go to Papa's house in the afterlife?" Baby James asked with a curious look on his face.

"One day son. One day," Triple J answered.

"Papa is with the ancestors now, in Orun Rere. That's the good heaven, where our true home is," Ashleigh explained to her son.

The three of them walked to their seats, while Triple J continued to stare at his father.

"You're home now," he said, kissing his father before going to his seat.

The home going service for Pastor James Johnson, Sr was star studded, packed with several of Triple J's celebrity friends. Two of them were listed on the program and sung the old man's favorite gospel songs. Turning the crowd out.

When Pastor Lee gave the eulogy, he had everyone and their Mama's standing up in the crowd praising God and the life of his friend.

"This is the day that the Lord has made, we will rejoice and be glad in it," he said, closing out.

As Pastor Lee walked off the stage, the church's choir sung. Next to Triple J he stood, creating small talk as the funeral home staff filed in. Wearing white suits with matching top hats, marched into the church high stepping to his casket. Once they were all in place they picked up the casket and raised it over their heads, marching out the same way they came in.

A horse drawn carriage waited for James Jay's body outside. Everyone that couldn't get in, recorded as the casket was carefully inserted into the glass carriage. Triple J and his family got into the black air-conditioned limousines to follow his father to the grave site.

"Your father was my friend, and I hate that he's gone. You know sometimes he would call me, and we would talk for hours about the Bible," Pastor Lee said, seated in the front seat.

"Yes, he was a good man," Triple J replied nonchalantly.

He knew his father was a righteous man and didn't care for the small talk. Pastor Lee claimed to be his friend but charged Triple J ten thousand dollars to host the funeral at his church, asking in the form of a donation.

That ain't no friend shit, Triple J thought. *I would have gave you more before you showed me it was all about money with you.*

Triple J sat in silence because nothing else mattered at the time. His priority was making sure his father's body was put in its resting place peacefully.

The police escorted them through the city, as crowds of onlookers recorded as the funeral passed.

"The whole wide world love Papa," Baby James said as he looked out of the window.

Triple J was humored by his son's way with words. It seemed like the whole wide world did love his father, especially those from their Grant Park community.

As the funeral procession pulled into the graveyard, butterflies filled his gut again. Looking to his ladies for support, Triple J grabbed both Ashleigh and Anastasia's hand. He struggled to maintain for his family, but tears began to flow heavily from his eyes.

"It's okay to cry daddy. When I hurt myself, I cry and when I get done, I feel better again," he said, hugging Triple J around the neck.

The family support he had, he couldn't have been more thankful for. The absence of his father had him weak, but he was thankful for his son.

"You know how to make daddy feel better," he said, squeezing Baby James back.

His father's body was already over the grave, by the time Triple J exited the limo. Pastor Lee and the other ministers spoke before releasing the white doves into the skies. Everyone watched them fly away, signifying his father's spirit going into the heavens. White roses were placed on top of his father's casket before they lowered him into the ground, by those close to him under the green funeral home tint.

As he was lowered into the ground, the tears of the ex-crime boss flowed from under his black designer shades.

"You're home now," Triple J whispered as he watched his father's casket lowered into the ground. "You're home now," he continued.

This Shit the Realest.

Chapter Twenty-Five

*T*wo days after the funeral of his father, Triple J met with the family's attorney to discuss their legal affairs. The house that he was raised in was in the family trust. Now that his father was gone, he wanted to square off some things.

"So, Ms. Stephanie, first I wanna say thank you for meeting with me on short notice. I'm here today because as you know my father has passed on. I came here today to go over his trust and respect his last wishes before rearranging the house," Triple J said.

"First, I want to give my condolences to you and your family. I know things must be hard losing your father," she said.

"He's in a better place now," Triple J replied, not wanting to get emotional.

"I understand. Well before you came, I looked over the documents. It's very clear that your father loved you and left all of his possessions in this trust to his one and only son. This will not be hard to deal with, once we get his death certificate, I'll file the estate documents with the state to transfer the property in Grant Park over and into your name," she continued.

Stephanie T. Lovelace Esq. was an attorney that practiced entertainment law. She represented several of Atlanta's Elite, managing their estates, an area she specialized in.

Triple J knew his father left him everything, but to cover his ass, he always consulted an attorney before making moves. When he was given all clear, he returned to his childhood residence with Ashleigh and Anastasia.

"We have to go through his things, to see what's worth keeping and what should be given away," he said to them.

As he unlocked the door to his old home, so many memories came back. Triple J showed them his old room with his old full-size bed still inside.

"I bet you used to have girls sneaking in and out of this window," Ashleigh said jokingly as she looked out.

"I didn't have to. It was just me and Pops here. I had my fun, but I wish I knew you two then, we would have had some fun on this bed," he said, making them both giggle.

"That would be nice," Anastasia said, smirking at the two of them.

Of the three, Anastasia loved the sex most, especially when they both gave him oral. Licking her lips she smiled at Ashleigh signaling to her that she was ready. Triple J knew they had a lot to go through but couldn't pass up on the opportunity.

The two ladies pooped everything off, swapping spit as they rubbed each other down. Joining the two, Triple J positioned himself behind Anastasia and he kissed on her neck, while fondling her breast. Melting in his arms, Anastasia's plump ass pushed into his lap, and she grinned on his dick. Triple J's penis instantly activated, and he was ready to perform.

Anastasia could feel his hard on penis, through the blue jean pants she wore. She continued to grind against him. Reaching her hand behind her back, she grabbed his rod and slowly slid her hand up and down his shaft while still kissing Ashleigh.

Ashleigh removed her clothes first, breaking the passionate kiss with her sister wife. Triple J smiled devilishly, while he prepared to sex his two ladies on the same bed that he lost his virginity.

Stripping down, he began to cock his rocket.

"Y'all bitches lucky y'all didn't know me back then. I would have gave you that Willie D," he whispered.

"Please, just give it to me," Ashleigh whispered back while licking her tongue around the rim of her lips.

Both ladies faced him kneeling at the edge of the bed. When Triple J reached them, Ashleigh was first to take him in her mouth. She slurped with him inside, twirling her tongue around in a circle. Her head game was phenomenal, and Triple J enjoyed the way she slobbers all over his knob.

"I don't think I would have been able to handle this as a kid," he said, complimenting them.

"I don't think you can handle us, as an adult," Anastasia shot back talking shit.

"See, that's where you got me fucked up at," Triple J said before beating on his chest.

Willie D had been activated, and he was back on his Ape Shit. Neither of them knew what to expect, still relaxed as he transformed. Anastasia was first to be demonized. King Ape flipped her over, like she was a rag doll onto her back. He held her legs into the air, like he was changing a diaper, before driving into her wet, warm and ready vagina.

Anastasia's eyes got buck in surprise, as she met the beast. Triple J began to heavily pound her pussy, like she had broken into his home.

"I'm so-orry!" She screamed. "I'm so-orry, da-addy," she continued.

Ashleigh laughed as she held Anastasia's hand.

"Girl, he putting a whooping on you," she said, chuckling.

"Help me?" Anastasia begged, squeezing Ashleigh's hand as she took his hard pipe.

Ashleigh felt sympathy for her sister and really tried to help. She began kissing on Triple J's abdomen trying to calm the handsome beast.

Once he started going Ape shit there wasn't much either of them could do for each other.

"Oh, you really just tried to help her? Now it's your turn," he said, pulling Ashleigh to him by the hair.

He threw her face first onto the bed, forced her head into the pillow, before he began tapping her ass from the back.

While pounding her pussy, Triple J stood up like he was trying to exit the other side.

"Oh shit, oh shit, oh shit," Ashleigh screamed as he nailed her to the bed.

Anastasia laughed as she laid on the side of her sister.

"Girl, I told you," Anastasia said, holding Ashleigh's hand.

Triple J had a lot of emotional stress build up from his father's passing and he took it out on them.

Exploding heavily inside of Ashleigh, he pumped all of his sperm into her warm love well.

"I'm the King Diggaling," he said while beating on his chest before he fell onto his back.

The explosion had taken a lot out of him, and he laid back between both of his ladies. Kissing them before they all fell asleep, Triple J thought, *This Shit the Realest.*

Chapter Twenty-Six

*A*wakened by the distinct ring tone on his phone, Triple J quickly got up. Both Ashleigh and Anastasia were still asleep, so he took the call in the next room.

"Tell me some good," he said, answering the phone.

"We need to meet asap. How long will it take for you to get to the city?" his private eye asked.

"I'm at the first headquarters," Triple J replied, referring to the Grant Park home.

"Come to the dugout," his private eye said before ending the call.

Triple J knew that if he was called to the dugout, there had to be some valuable information being exchanged. As a precaution, he grabbed the keys to Anastasia's Range Rover not wanting to be spotted.

"I'll be back," he said, kissing them both before getting dressed.

"Be careful," Ashleigh replied, voice filled with concern.

Since being released from prison, Triple J took extra precautions when dealing with the streets. The dugout was one of the original Ape's club houses where members gambled and got wasted with hot sexy ladies. It got its moniker, from its unique location off the road and in the cut.

Triple J passed the dugout twice, checking his mirrors to make sure he wasn't being followed. When he felt all was clear, he spent the block pulling into the back parking lot before he parked.

"I'm outside," Triple J said, calling for the door.

"Alright," the man replied.

Triple J looked around Anastasia's car and found a black bedazzled face mask in her armrest, one she wore during Covid. He put it on and threw on his black hoodie and shades before getting out of the truck.

As soon as he reached the back door, the locks were removed and the door was slightly opened, enough for him to enter.

"They're in the back," the doorman said.

Triple J knew his way around the dugout well; it was one of those places his dad held down back in the days. As soon as he entered the back room, he saw a beautiful black female bound to a single chair with tears flowing from her eyes. She looked like she'd been beaten in the face, and he knew the cause.

"Oh my gosh who did this to her?" Triple J asked, pulling the cloth from around her mouth, sounding as if he genuinely cared. "I'm sorry about this ma'am. Would you like some water?" He asked.

She shook her head up and down signaling to him that she would.

"Okay! So, I see that my first generous gesture was taken for granted. I thought when I took the bound from around your mouth, you would be able to speak," he said to her flipping out, going low key crazy. "My next plan was to remove the straps from around your legs so that you can walk out of here on your own, but I see you don't like acts of generosity," he said, removing his glasses, hoodie and mask exposing his face. "Before you start lying to me, let's get one thing clear, I don't care if you live or die. I'm only here to find out the truth," he said to her. "What role did you play in my uncle's death?"

"I don't know your uncle, Triple J. I promise," she said, screaming in tears.

"Strike 2," he said, staring into her eyes with a sinister look.

Triple J shook his head up and down full of excitement as he thought about the bullet he was about to put in her head.

"You see the only game my father ever let me play growing up was baseball. This is one of those cases when you're under a lot of pressure. It's the bottom of the ninth, bases loaded and you're at bat. You have 2 strikes against you and if you get one more you're out and your team loses," he stares at her for a brief second. "See what that means is that if you strike out, I'm gonna put a bullet in your head. Now what role did you play in my uncle's murder?" He asked for a second time.

"I'm not sure who your uncle is," she replies with heavy tears flowing from her eyes.

"He was murdered at Fairfield State Prison," Triple J said.

A light bulb went off in her head and a surprise look filled her eyes. Triple J knew then that he was about to get the information that he yearned so much for.

"You have something you want to tell me?" He asked.

"It was that fed lady that visited my son. She said she could get him and my husband out if they did a favor for her." The bound woman said.

"Who is your son?" Triple J asked.

"His name is Kahlil," she replied, taking a heavy gulp.

That name didn't ring a bell as wasn't one of the guys that went down for Stacks murder. Triple J thought for a second, but nothing rung to him.

"Is he at Fairfield?" Triple J asked.

"No, he's in the feds," she replied. "My husband is at Fairfield."

"What's his name?" Triple J asked.

"Thomas, but they call him..."

"G Code!" Triple J said, interrupting her.

So, the whole time this nigga supposed to been finding out who killed Unc and he's the one," Triple J thought.

G Code had not lived up to his name, violating the Gangsters Code and working for the feds. Under normal circumstances, women and children were off limits, but since G Code played the game, raw there were no boundaries.

While they were inside, Triple J remembered G Code bragging about a woman named Sugar. He claimed she would be his ticket out the hood giving him a new life.

"Your man took something from me and now I must even the score. Nice to meet you Sugar," Triple J said before pulling a gun from his waistband and putting a bullet in her head.

This Shit the Realest.

Chapter Twenty-Seven

*A*fter settling the score with G Code, Triple J took several precautionary measures, to ensure that he kept his freedom.

A cleaning crew was called to clean the dugout from front to back, leaving no trace of the deceased woman. Triple J drove himself to one of his duck off spots, the one he used to sterilize himself after a job.

The blood spatter and brain matter got all over him and his clothes so to be cautious he dropped them in a tub of acid. Using a burner phone, he messaged Ashleigh, directing her to lock up his father's house and meet him back at the ranch.

As he drove home his mind raced as he thought about the evening's events.

This nigga played me, smiling in my face the whole time, Triple J thought referring to G-Code.

Anastasia and Baby James greeted him with smiles and hugs as he walked through the door.

"Hey Daddy," Baby James screamed running to his dad

after Triple J and Anastasia kissed. "Daddy, you know I'm the world's luckiest kid," Baby James said.

"How is that?" Triple J asked his son.

"Because, only the worlds luckiest kid has two mommies," he continued rocking back and forth, as he held Anastasia's hand.

Ashleigh's spiritual radar went off, when she walked in the room, feeling the negative energy fueling off of him.

Protecting her family, Ashleigh grabbed Triple J's hand and drug him to her spiritual space, a room near the back of their home. Along the walls were several spiritual altars, representing the African orishas. Triple J rarely visited her space but, from previous experience, he remembered to greet Esu first, knocking three times on the floor before entering.

Ashleigh followed behind him, walking to one of the altars on the far side of the room. Triple J sat down on a white mat and watched her as she grabbed a glass gallon jug with a dark colored liquid inside.

"You took someone's life tonight," she said as she poured the protection oil on top of his head. "Your ori is in a mess right now and spirit says, 'You have to make ebo," she said to him.

Triple J wasn't surprised that she knew. Deep down, he was thankful to have her in his life because during crucial times, she had his back.

"Tomorrow, we have to get a bucket of lard and a bucket of cowrie shells. Spirit wants two pigeons from you, and half a dozen eggs. You seeking vengeance for your uncle's death is hurting you, but since you're so persistent, I'm going to ask spirit to show you everything," Ashleigh said.

"Thank you," Triple J said, staring into her eyes.

Ashleigh made a spiritual concoction for him mixed with different herbs. She heated hot water in her tea pot and poured it into a wooden bowl.

"Drink it," she said, holding the bowl up to his mouth.

Triple J drank the potion and passed out before he was halfway finished.

You poisoned me, he thought as he fell to the floor.

The loud Bantu drumbeats woke him, and he quickly rose to his feet. Triple J realized that he was no longer in his home, but out on the streets. Looking down at his torn garments, he realized that he was a bum out on the streets.

Damn, she poisoned me and took everything I had, he thought as the rage inside of his body brewed.

As he explored the area that he was in, things began to look familiar. Recognizing the waterfall landmark, Triple J realized that he was standing outside of Houston's Granduca Hotel, the same one he and his wife stayed at before his arrest.

Looking to make an aid and assist call to one of his homies, Triple J walked towards the hotel's main entrance. As he neared the doors, he spotted his ex-wife Jessica and her cousin Bianca hugging outside of their car.

Not wanting to be seen in his torn garments, Triple J hid himself behind a concrete pillar.

"We'll plan something better next time," Bianca said before kissing her cousin on the cheek.

Jessica waited on the curb as Bianca got back into the car.

"Alright, I love you B. Text me and let me know you made it in safely," Jessica said as she pulled away.

Triple J began to follow her as she walked inside.

Things got weird when he saw a woman tailing her that resembled his mom.

"What is my mom doing here?" He asked himself.

Triple J tried to follow them inside, but the hotel's security stopped him.

"You need to leave before I call Houston PD," the security officer said to him rudely.

"I have a room here," he said.

"Not in them rags," the valet attendant jokes.

Triple J saw his reflection in the glass door and coward down, before turning away.

I gotta find a way inside, he thought as he walked back to the sidewalk.

Familiar with commercial real estate, he walked towards the rear of the building looking for the delivery dock. As soon as he bent the corner, he saw several federal agents dressing into their tactical gear.

What the hell? This the same crew that arrested me, he thought looking at them.

Afraid of being spotted, Triple J hid behind the trash can as they geared up.

"He's in the Executive Suites room 1812," the woman that favored his mom said jumping off the back dock.

The tactical unit grabbed their helmets and weapons before they marched one after the other inside. Triple J kneeled lower behind the dumpster, trying to stay out of sight, but lost his footing and fell against the metal container letting off a loud echo.

"Who's over there?" The woman asked quickly, pulling out her service weapon.

She clicked on her weapon's attached flashlight and began walking towards him. Triple J heard her steps and tried to reverse step towards the rear of the dumpster, but she quickly bent the corner, scaring the shit out of him.

His hands flew in the air as he stared down the barrel of her Glock 10mm.

"I'm so sorry sir," she said, holstering her weapon. "You don't have to go through the trash, I'll give you something to eat," she said, waving him to come out.

Triple J didn't like the police and wanted to walk away, but his stomach was touching his back. From the passenger seat of her Tahoe, she grabbed a to-go container and handed it to him. Triple J gladly accepted the leftover plate; from the restaurant she'd just run surveillance on Jessica and Bianca at.

When he opened the container, his eyes lit up and he began eating the food with his hands, before her two-way radio went off.

"Shots fired, shots fired," a male voice screamed into the radio.

"Hold your fire! Hold your fire! We need him alive," she yelled back into her radio, quickly grabbing it from her beltline.

"Sorry, I gotta go," she said before giving him a wink and taking off running towards the dock.

As she departed, Triple J began to wake up.

When he came to, the lights were off, and a $100 dollar bill was burning on a plate in front of him. Directly behind the flame was a picture of his mom and another woman that mirrored her.

"Where did you get this picture?" Triple J asked, half awake.

"In the photo album at your dads house," Ashleigh replied.

Until then, Triple J never knew his mom had a twin sister. As he sat on the white mat, he wondered why his father never showed him the photo of his mother and her sister.

He had so many questions, he wished could be answered, if his father was now deceased.

"So, how was it?" Ashleigh asked.

Triple J stared at her and shook his head in total confusion.

"Something's not right. We need to go see my uncle for clarity," Triple J answered as he stood from the floor.

This Shit the Realest.

Chapter Twenty-Eight

*T*he next morning after breakfast, Triple J and Ashleigh left for the botanical to retrieve materials needed for his ebo sacrifice. Waking up with a lot of unanswered questions racing through his mind, he sat silent the entire morning not saying a word to anyone.

"You know I love you and I'm here with you forever," Ashleigh said showing her love and support.

Triple J looked at her briefly with no emotion in his eyes, before he returned his eyes to the road.

"What's wrong with you James," she asked, grabbing a hold of his free hand.

He ignored her and continued to drive, not saying a word.

"I am not doing this with you. Stop the car and let me out," she said, grabbing her purse from the floor.

He continued to drive as she fueled in anger.

"I said, stop the fucking car," she screamed at him.

Triple J had never heard her yell, let alone get upset

with him. He pulled the truck over to the side of the road and looked at her.

"If I let you out, where are you gonna go," he asked her as she opened the door.

"Oh, so now you can talk?" She asked him.

"It's a lot going on up here right now, I'm just trying to figure it all out," he said resting his hand on his head.

"Bottling up your pain hurts you and everyone else. Before we left the house, Baby James asked if you were okay because you wouldn't answer him. I'm always here for you, but before I accept being ignored, I'll get out of this car and find me a man that knows communication is the key to every relationship," she said.

Triple J stared at her and still words wouldn't come out of his mouth.

"Okay that's it," she said, opening the truck's door and stepping her right foot out.

"Hold up," Triple J said, staring at her as tears filled his eyes. "Don't leave. I need you, Ashleigh," he continued.

"And! I need you to talk, James!" She shouted back.

"Okay! Just get in the truck," he said in a calm tone.

She returned inside and closed the door. Triple J grabbed his woman by the hand and looked directly into her eyes.

"Growing up, my father taught me to live a certain way. He told me; to survive in this game called life, I must never let my right hand know what my left is doing. I didn't think that rule applied to me and him, but I see it did," Triple J said.

"What is it, James?" Ashleigh asked, squeezing his hand.

"I grew up by myself as a kid, no brother, no sister, no cousins, it was just me and my Pops. He was in the streets, and I followed, so the streets became the only family that I knew. I asked him if I had any family on my mother's side and he only told me about my one uncle in Cuba. This whole time, he knew my mama had a twin sister but held that from me. Last night when you put me under that spell, I returned to the night of my Houston arrest. I was homeless and, on the street, outside of the hotel when I saw everything that happened that night. My mom's sister is a Fed, and she ran the whole show," Triple J said, turning to look out the driver's window. "I feel like my whole life has been a lie and now I don't know who to trust," he continued.

"I have something to tell you," Ashleigh said.

"Don't tell me you knew the whole time," Triple J said looking back at Ashleigh.

"No! But when we were looking through the photo album at your father's house, I grabbed the picture because I recognized the woman from the plane," she said.

"How do you remember her, when you see millions of passengers?" He asked.

"Because she paid me to have sex with you," Ashleigh said, dropping a bombshell.

"Paid you!" He yelled. "So, you're in on this shit to?" He asked, truly upset.

"It wasn't like that," she yelled back at him, as tears filled her eyes.

"Well, how the fuck was it. Cuz right now, all I can see is that I've been manipulated and violated.

"Violated?" She spat back at him.

"Yeah, Bitch! Don't act like you didn't rape me on that plane. And what's more fucked up about all of this, I'm over here thinking we have something real, but you're just the airline whore," he yelled slicing her with his words. "If I knew this, I would have been your pimp and let you sell that lil pussy for me since you are selling it," he continued to yell.

"Oh my God, James!" she screamed before the bottom of her face fell off and tears poured from her eyes.

Triple J realized at that very moment that he'd fucked up bad. Although she was a strong and spiritual woman her face showed heartbreak and humiliation. Although she had kept secrets from him, Ashleigh was his best friend, and he actually loved her. The new information she'd given him was enough to drive any man crazy, especially one from the streets.

Triple J knew he'd come too far to go soft on her now.

"You wanted me to talk, now let's fucking talk. Why did you do it?" He asked, yelling at the top of his lungs.

Ashleigh couldn't speak. She had bald up in her seat weeping, with her hands covering her face.

"You wanted to talk so bad, now let's talk. Got dammit. Why did you lie to me?" He asked again. "First, you raped me. Then, you made me think you really love me. But the whole time it's been for some fucking money," he spat at her.

"I do love you and it's not about money," she said, pausing to catch her breath. "You could have lost it all and I still would be here for you, James. We have a child together," she yelled back at him.

"Yeah! Fuck all that. Why did you do it?" He asked again.

"For my dad," she screamed. "I did it for my dad."

"What you mean?" He asked.

"At the time, he was ill, and I was working all of the

overtime so that I could to pay his medical bills. Your aunt offered me thirty thousand in cash to have sex with you. At first, I turned it down, but when I saw who she was talking about, my pussy got instantly wet. I had fell in love with the man I saw and thirty thousand made me want you more. I knew I could lure you away from the Marshall's and thought you would want some pussy before you went in. Thirty thousand and some good dick from the good-looking man I had to do it," she said.

Triple J thought about what she'd said for a second before responding.

"So, is that why you said in your letter that you saw something special in me, before you know who I was?" He asked.

"No! I really did. The lady on the plane just solidified what I was already thinking when she offered me the money," Ashleigh continued.

"So, if we could go back to that day, would you have still raped me if there was no money involved?" He asked.

"I would have been your cellmate," she said, kissing him.

Triple J laughed but knew the love was real with her. Although she'd hurt him, he was thankful that she was in his life. There were still questions that needed to be answered and his uncle in Cuba was the only one that could give them.

This Shit the Realest.

Chapter Twenty-Nine

*S*ince meeting with Triple J's uncle, Donjuan had been working as his concierge. Last he heard, DonJuan's business was booming without him present, and he was back and forth between countries.

Looking to get in contact with his uncle, Triple J called his buddy's cell phone twice, but there was no answer.

"Damn, I gotta get down there to see Unk," Triple said aloud.

"Where is he?" Ashleigh asked, seated next to him on the sofa.

"Cuba," he replied.

"So, what's the problem?" she asked.

"I need to contact the pilot, but I can't because my potna has the satellite phone," he replied.

"Daddy, did you forget that I work for the airlines?" She asked.

"I did, but this is different. I can't fly into Cuba's international to get to him. I have to land on a private air strip and his soldiers will carry me from there," he said.

"I can make it happen," Ashleigh said, pulling out her phone making a call.

As she talked to the person on the phone, Triple J's mind wondered.

It just doesn't make sense. Why have they kept this a secret from me for so long, he thought.

As his mind raced, Ashleigh ended her call.

"So, I have us a gulf stream that's fully operator-able, but label decommissioned. One of my favorite pilots, Alex Alexander is an ex-Marine with over 100 thousand hours in the air. He's agreed to fly us roundtrip at no cost, answering a favor he owes me," she said.

"Airline Ashleigh to the rescue," Triple J said before kissing her.

"We're wheels up in an hour," she said before leaving the room.

Three hours away, Anastasia drove them to a private airport where they boarded the black Gulf stream. It sat in a hanger of its own near the far side of the airport.

Once they got on board, Triple J gave the pilot the wrong coordinates just in case someone was watching their flight manifest. He knew they had to be cautious in every way.

After all of his safety checks, the pilot had them wheels up in no time. Triple J rested his head on the cushioned seat and let out a heavy exhale breath.

"Are you okay?" Ashleigh asked.

"Naw, but I will be," he said looking out of the window.

Ashleigh reclined his seat and sat on his lap facing him. She laid her head on his chest, her place of comfort.

"It's going to be okay," she said, putting his arms around her waist.

Triple J held her in his arms and together they fell asleep.

Awakened by the plane's turbulence, Triple J hugged Ashleigh tighter in his arms.

"Sorry about that," the pilot said. "We just entered Cuba's air space," he continued.

Triple J laid Ashleigh on the chair next to his and walked to the cockpit. Showing him a small map, he pointed to a heavily wooded area far west of the original location.

"We're going to land here," he said, pointing at the true landing zone.

"We will not be able to put it down here," Alex said to him looking at the map's terrain markings.

"Trust me. The maps look that way, but that's where we're going," he said, changing the flight course.

When they got there, the pilot could see the hidden private strip. It looked heavily wooded from the skies, but it was definitely there. Inaudible Spanish was shouted into the radio by someone from the ground.

"They're saying we will be killed if we land here," the pilot said translating their message into English.

There shouldn't be any radio traffic out here, Triple J thought.

He didn't know who was speaking, but he knew when they hit the ground, he would be taken to his uncle.

"Land the plane. We'll deal with them down there," Triple J said.

Once they were on the ground heavily armed men surrounded the plane with assault rifles pointed at them.

"Ah, Triple J," Alex called to him. "We have a bit of a problem," he continued.

Alex was ex-military and he'd been in several war zones. He knew that the guys on the ground were rural rebels and had very little training. Outgunned twenty to none, he looked at Triple J with the look of, you better know what you're doing.

"It's cool they're the escorts to my uncle," he said in a calm tone.

As soon as they opened the hatch door, the men raced towards them screaming in Spanish. A jeep was parked in front of the plane with a .50 Cal mounted on the back.

Triple J stepped up first, with his hands above his head. In his hand was a hand drawn picture of the pendant, he would have presented if DonJuan didn't have it.

"I'm here to see Hefe," he said, before he was knocked out by the ass end of an AK-47.

The rocky dirt road woke him, as he bounced around in the back of the pick-up truck. His hands and feet were bound together, and a fabric sack had him hoodwinked.

Damn, this shit hurts, he thought as he slammed against the truck bed jumping off holes in the road.

When the road smoothed and all of the bouncing ceased, he knew they had made it to his uncle's property.

"We're here," Triple J heard someone say when the truck stopped.

Multiple footsteps could be heard walking along the side of the truck. When the tailgate opened, Triple J was drugged by his feet and dropped to the ground. The air was knocked out of him and his dizziness intensified.

"Let me see their faces, before you take them out back," an unrecognized male voice said.

Removing Ashleigh's and Alex's mask first, he didn't

recognize either of them. After Triple J's mask was removed, he immediately dropped to his knees to help his friend. DonJuan looked at the henchmen with a worried look in his eyes and they knew they had fucked up.

This Shit the Realest.

Chapter Thirty

he infirmary sat on the west wing of the palace, near the royal family's luxurious living quarters. As a security precaution, only approved family and veteran staff members were allowed inside while Triple J's ill uncle received treatment.

"Arhh," Triple J moaned as he came to.

His eyes were in a blur and his arm was hooked to an IV. He looked around the room, searching for his fiancé and when he didn't see her, he called her name.

"Ashleigh!" He called. "Ash," He continued.

The live-in nurse heard his distress calls and rushed to his bedside.

"She's okay señor, Ms. Ashleigh is in the next room," she said, speaking with a Hispanic accent.

"Bring her to me," he demanded.

"I'm sorry señor. I can't do that. Security rules," she replied to him.

"Well, take me to her. I need to know she's okay," he continued.

"I can do that señor," she replied with a smile.

She rolled the wheelchair to Triple J's bedside, assisting him into his seat.

"You come all the way to Cuba and forget all about your old man?" he heard a male's voice say from the opposite side of the medical divider.

"Uncle Javier?" Triple J asks.

"Yeah, this me," he said with a chuckle, before he began to cough heavily.

Triple J could hear the pain in his coughs.

"Are you alright?" He asked as the nurse rolled him around the divider next to his uncle's bed.

"Yeah, there's nothing a little water can't fix," he replied before sipping from the glass cup. "You're looking good son," his Uncle Javier continued.

King Javier Ikembe was the youngest brother to Triple J's maternal grandfather and since age thirty-eight, he's held the grand position over the western world. Although he was terminally ill in his later years, he was still sharper than a Swiss army knife, capable of making well calculated decisions.

"Sock it to me," he said, bumping fist with his only nephew.

The Ikembe family stemmed off the African Royal bloodline and secretly reigned over Cuba. Legend has it, Baba Benji Ikembe, heir to the Oyo kingdom in West Africa, was captured and sold into slavery during his early adult years. Trained in African martial arts, he used the unique style of fighting and defeated his Spanish masters, gaining freedom for himself and the other African slaves in their area. Secretly managing the plantation over the other slaves, Baba Benji became a silent ruler. Free from Spanish conquers he made a way for the Ikembe dynasty to continue in the new land.

With skin darker than the midnight skies, Baba Benji knew the rest of the world wouldn't trade with him. He made an agreement with the lighter skinned mix-breed slaves, later known as the Esco Family, to sell them their harvested cocaine.

For generations the agreement was kept until Diablo Esco the great grandson gained power over his family. He thought the Ikembe family was weak because they hid in the woods and waged war, after Triple J's grandfather's untimely death.

What Diablo didn't know was that Javier Ikembe was sent abroad to a European university for mercenaries and there he became best friends with a kid whose father was Director of the American CIA.

Using his American contacts, Javier defeated the Esco men, killing Diablo and his four sons without ever touching a gun or sword.

"It's your network that determines your net worth," Javier said, telling Triple J how he gained the moniker Javier the Great.

The green and red bracelet on Triple J's wrist got his uncle's attention.

"I see you've found your way back to your roots," he said looking at his wrist.

"This," he paused, looking down at the bracelet. "My fiancé, Ashleigh, gave it to me. She said it's for a long life," Triple J continued.

"Asè. Do you think she's worthy of the Ikembe last name," he asked before coughing heavily again.

Triple J thought about his question before giving an answer.

Before he could, the nurse rushed to King Javier's bedside, assisting him with another glass of water.

"Your uncle is very sick and needs to rest," she said to Triple J, "Maybe, we come back," she continued, speaking in a broken accent.

Javier nodded his head for Triple J to go, giving him time to catch his breath.

"Ms. Ashleigh?" The nurse asked as she rolled him out of the door, into the hallway.

Triple J nodded his head, ready to see his fiancé. As soon as they turned the corner, his mother's twin sister approached them from the opposite end of the hallway. Triple J almost didn't recognize her, dressed in her royal robes, accompanied by three of her lady servants. She signaled for the nurse to stop his chair, and she stood him up wrapping her arms around his neck.

"Oh my God! I've been waiting your entire life for this moment nephew," she said as tears filled her eyes.

Triple J could feel the love radiating through her embrace but couldn't give it back. He didn't know her like that and there was an unhealthy amount of mind-boggling questions he had for her.

"I love you so much," she continued as tears flowed from her eyes.

As she they stared at each other, he felt weird because she was a living image of pictures he had of his deceased mother. Pinching himself as if he was in a dream, Triple J quickly realized that This Shit the Realest

Chapter Thirty-One

*a*t 6 o'clock on the dot, the supper bell rang for the family in the dining room. Triple J and Ashleigh met with his aunt and uncle at the dining table, in their royal dress.

"So glad you could join us this evening," his aunt said, addressing Ashleigh.

"I'm honored to be here," she replied.

"The Doctor didn't want to let your uncle leave the infirmary, but you know your Uncle Javier," his aunt said.

"I've listened to that doctor for four years now. I wouldn't miss dinner with my nephew for any Doctor in this world," he continued.

"Thank you, Uncle Javier. I'm honored to be amongst family. Especially since my father's death," Triple J replied.

"How has that been for you?" Uncle Javier asked.

Triple J paused for a second not really sure how to answer.

"Things are things," he humbly replied.

"What kind of answer is that?" His Aunt asked.

"It's the best that I have at the moment," Triple J shot back at her, getting upset.

"Alright, now. Let's all be transparent here. We're family and if there's anything that needs to be worked out now is the time to lay it on the table," his uncle said before a heavy wave of coughs.

"Okay then, let's talk about the real reason I'm here. My father's best friend was murdered in front of me while I was in prison. I've hired private investigators, and all roads have led me here. Can you explain to me why?" Triple J asked.

Ashleigh adjusted herself in the chair next to him as they prepared for a response to come.

"When you were a baby, we got a heartbreaking call that my sister was killed in a drive by shooting. The shooters were a part of a drug distribution ring that were rivals of your father's called the Miami Boys. Your father assigned Stacks, to protect your mom while she shopped for household goods. He failed to do so, leaving my sister riddled in bullets on the ground covering her only child. That day you were shot in the hand," she said answering Triple J's lifelong question for the scare on his hand. "Stacks answered by killing several of their top leaders in revenge, which wasn't enough for your grandfather. After seeing your mother's body, he asked me to make sure the man that failed to protect his daughter dies with more holes in his body than your mother did," Triple J's aunt said staring him directly in the eyes.

"Why was I told that my mother died while giving birth to me?" Triple J asked.

"That's the story your father gave you? It's my guess, he didn't want you to seek revenge against his friend once you became of age," his aunt answered.

"Why didn't you come and tell me the truth?" Triple J asked.

"Because we needed you. When Stacks got arrested, he was sentenced to life without parole plus 400 years. We lost him in the system and when we pressed your Baba for information on him, he gave us very little. We sent guys into the prisons, but no one ever got close enough to take him. We made multiple attempts, and you were our last result," she continued.

"Well why did no one ever tell me what was happening?" Triple J asked.

"Stacks a real killer and he would have felt you there. He mastered the prison world, and he would have killed you before you got a chance to.

"It all makes sense, Triple J said. "Stacks survived for so long at Fairfield because he screened everyone that came in. When I got there, he put me in the cell next to his, not to protect me, but to watch me."

Keep your friends close, but your enemies closer, Triple J thought about his father's teachings.

"So how long have y'all been planning this?" Triple J asked.

"Since the day we forced your father to retire and you took over the family business," Uncle Javier answered.

Triple J never underestimated his uncle. He knew the old man was trained for combat and his war strategies were so tactical that he could write a book.

"So, this whole thing was a set up. Y'all almost killed me in the process," Triple J said.

"That was an accident, and I was there the entire time," his aunt said. "How do you think you met Ashleigh?" She asked.

"Oh, I know," Triple J replied. "You paid her 30k to rape me on that plane."

"What about Captain James and Lt. Rodgers? You think they risked their lives for a criminal? There were plenty of incentives for you. I made sure you had everything you needed and wanted. The fall was an accident, but perfect for the plan. It made it all more genuine," she continued.

"So, it was you that was pulling strings behind the scenes. When I came out of the coma, the streets were saying that I was cooperating with the law," he said.

"Yes, it was me. The same me, that got all of your guys off the RICO."

"I bet that was hard for you, when you put us there," Triple J interrupted.

"All honestly, I had no idea that JT Wolf was an undercover detective. After he and Jessica started secretly spending a lot of time together, I had my people look deep into him. He and the DA's office were working behind our back to bring down the entire ANW instead of just you. I went and talked with Jessica about him, and my best guess is that she told him about our conversation. We assumed she spotted me in Houston and connected the dots to me and the agency. That's how he got the federal cooperation idea about you," she said.

As she talked, Triple J listened, and his life began to make sense. He looked to Ashleigh for her input. The look in her eyes let him know that the story his aunt gave corroborated with spirit.

Caught up in the heat of the moment, everyone forgot that King Javier was seated at the table. When Triple J looked towards him, he knew immediately that the old man was gone by the blank stare in his eyes. Although he didn't smile much, the expression on his face let them know that he was in heavenly peace.

Javier's sudden death left the Ikembe Dynasty unruled. With no children, nor siblings alive, the kingdom was to be given to the next eldest male with Ikembe blood.

Triple J didn't know how to respond, when his aunt stood from her chair and began to bow before.

"All hail to our new King James Ikembe," she said loud enough for everyone in the house to hear before knocking three times at his feet.

This Shit the Realest.

Chapter Thirty-Two

$\mathcal{B}$efore traveling to Cuba, to get answers for Stacks murder, Triple J didn't expect to become King of the Ikembe Dynasty. Forced to stay in Cuba, while several projects were going on back home, he was thankful to have Anastasia state side. Using her as his eyes, she oversaw the construction of The Executive Homies Farm Academy.

From Monday thru Saturday, construction crews worked on their home property. Facing timing Anastasia and Baby James daily, Triple J was able to see the progress that they were making all the way in Cuba.

"How's everything coming?" Ashleigh asked one afternoon, while they waited for brunch.

"Omg Bae, they're making it look so easy out there. The building structure for the horse barn has gone up and they've started putting the doors on the supply storage," she said, showing them on the phone.

"Oh wow!" Ashleigh said in amazement as she watched

her idea come to life over the phone. "They are moving fast," she continued.

Now that he was king, Triple J had an unlimited supply of financial resources at hand. He paid double the workers' salaries, to get them working six days a week, instead of their normal five. The goal was to get construction done sooner than the projected deadline, so that he could hold another event.

As a community service project, Triple J had several of The Executive Homie's mentees participate in the construction project. Giving them a position in the educational academy being built for them.

"I see Michael and Trayvon are out there," Triple J said after spotting them in a photo Anastasia sent.

"Yes, I talked with them yesterday. They are loving the educational experience out there, learning as much as they can. Michael wanted me to tell you that he was with the welders yesterday and really liked it. He showed me the weld he did, I guess it was good because the welders praised him for stacking nickels," she replied.

Hearing the word stack, reminded him of his father's late best friend.

All of this time, Uncle Javier knew that he was dying but didn't until he knew that Stacks was gone. Although Stacks failed at protecting my mother, he sacrificed himself to protect me. For that reason alone, he must be honored, Triple J thought.

Ashleigh and Anastasia continued to talk, catching up with each other while he checked on their other business.

"You know your family really loves you, James. The whole time I was with your uncle, all he did was brag about you," DonJuan said.

Triple J studied him as he talked and went into thought.

"This whole time you knew?" Triple J asked, eyes locked on his.

"I was told to withhold certain things from you, on behalf of the Ikembe family," DonJuan replied in a professional tone.

Triple J's mind went back to the conversation he had with DonJuan when he first got to Fairfield.

"Are you good down there?" DonJuan asked.

"It's prison and I know it could be worse, but I think I'm good. My dad's best friend Stacks is down here, and he's got the camp on lock," Triple J replied.

That's how they knew when I made contact with him, he thought.

"On behalf of the Ikembe family I thank you," King James replied in a royal tone.

"Your Highness, May I have a word with you?" Ashleigh asked, intercepting their conversation.

Triple J followed her back to their living quarters, wondering what was so important.

"What going on?" He asked.

"Your son wants to see you," she said, turning the computer towards him.

"Baby James! What's going on, son?" Triple J asked with a smile on his face as he walked towards the laptop.

"I'm not Baby James no more daddy. I'm the Prince," he said, correcting his father.

"You're right son. You are the prince," Triple J replied.

"Now, you gotta start over daddy," he said.

"Prince James! What's going on, son?" Triple J asked with a chuckle.

"I'm just cooling it," he replied, throwing up the peace sign and nodding his head up and down.

Both Triple J and Anastasia laughed at their son.

"Where you get that from?" Triple J asked him while laughing.

"One of the contractors. He does that every time he sees James," Anastasia replied.

He's growing up on me, so fast. By the time I get back home, he'll be driving, Triple J thought.

"When are you coming home? Because Mama real sick," Prince James asked.

"I told you I'm good James," Anastasia said, cutting him off. "Why did you tell your father that?" She said getting onto him.

"What do you mean, she's sick?" Triple J asked his son.

"I'm good Daddy. It's nothing for you to worry about," she replied to him.

"No Daddy. Mommie always be throwing up," he said, bussing her out.

Ashleigh overheard them and quickly returned to the computer. She looked at Anastasia from over Triple J's shoulder and saw the slight difference in her face.

"When one person dies, another is born," Ashleigh said with a smile.

Anastasia dropped her head before she started crying. When she looked up, she shook her head up and down with a smile.

"Are you?" Triple J asked.

"Yes!" Anastasia replied with a smile. "We're pregnant!" She continued.

Joy had filled all of their hearts, as they thought about

the growing seed inside of her. Although the pregnancy wasn't planned, it fitted right into his plan.

Smiling from ear-to-ear Triple J was excited to be expecting their next child.

This Shit the Realest.

Chapter Thirty-Three

Seven months after finding out about his expected seed, Triple J had to make his way home. Traveling arrangements took longer now that he was King James Ikembe. He had to travel with an entire staff of forty plus from cooks to security. Entering the states, everyone had to have passports and Visas, and they took time to get.

Anastasia's belly had grown as big as their house. She still was able to plan the grand opening of The Executive Homies, School of Agricultural and Farming.

Like before, Triple J gave her full access to everything that she needed and allowed her and Ashleigh to create the guest list together.

"How are you feeling, love?" Triple J asked while rubbing around her stomach.

"I feel like an old lady. These twins got my back hurting," she said.

"Please, have a seat?" he asked her.

"I'm good. They're just in here flipping around, like American Ninja Warriors," she said with a chuckle.

Triple J was extremely excited, when he found out they were having a set of twins. The medical doctor labeled her pregnancy high risk and that pushed them to hire an African midwife to help her get through it all.

For months, Triple J planned a surprise for the two of them. He sent them to a seamstress, to customize gowns for the grand opening. When the dresses were delivered, tears flowed from their eyes when they saw the bedazzled white wedding gowns.

"I wish I could kick your butt," Ashleigh said, calling him on the phone.

"I wish I could kiss yours," he replied sexually.

"You're so slick," Anastasia said. "You let us plan our own wedding, without us even knowing it was our wedding being planned," she stated.

"Once the divorce with Jessica was finalized, I didn't want to wait any longer," he replied. "I know wedding planning can be stressful and that's not what our family needs. The two of you are my joy and my peace. Together, you mean the most to me. Today the three of us will become one, both King and Queens, living happily ever after like in the movies," he said to them.

"Aww that was so cute, but save it for your vows," Anastasia said, making all of them laugh.

"You could have told us. I don't even have anyone to walk me down the aisle," Ashleigh said since her father had died.

"Yes, you do. He should be knocking on your door, right, about, now," Triple J said right as the first tap knock on the door.

When Ashleigh opened the door, her jaw dropped to the floor in surprise.

"Tunde," she screamed, jumping towards her brother, hugging him around the neck.

After he took care of the business with G Code on the inside, Triple J promised to get him out. Seeing Tunde clean himself up, Triple J was proud of the progress his brother-in-law made. He'd gained weight and his skin had the fresh out of prison glow. His arms were muscular toned, bulging out the sleeves of his suit. He made sure to get his suit fitted showing off his muscular physique.

"I kept my word that I would get clean, and James kept his," Tunde said to his sister.

"Alright now, you see her. Let them get ready and I'll catch you outside," Triple J said, putting him out of his wife's room.

While the hair and makeup ladies dolled up his ladies, Triple J and a few of his homies caught up. He listened to them as they talked about all of their community endeavors. Although he didn't say much, his smile let them all know that he was happy.

We left a multi-million-dollar crime organization, to successful black male entrepreneurs. We're having everything now from commercial real estate to custom T-Shirts, hats and sport slides. I make sure my team eat. Now, that's my definition of a King," he thought.

The wedding guests were called to their seats, once the ladies were ready. Triple J and his groomsmen stood at the altar in their royal dress attire next to the ceremonial priest. As soon as the music began to play and he saw his soon to be wives file into the aisle, tears filled the eyes of the King.

Anastasia's father disagreed with their poly marriage and refused to walk his daughter down the aisle to Triple J. Surprising the crowd, Ashleigh decided that she would walk with Anastasia to signify their sister bond.

They are so beautiful, Triple J thought as they walked towards him.

Once they reached the altar, Triple J stepped down and they each grabbed one of his arms, escorted to their places on the stage.

"We gather here today, to unite King James Ikembe and his wives to be, Ashleigh and Anastasia," their priest said, beginning the ceremony.

They all had nervous looks in their eyes as the ceremony went on, although they were sure of their marriage. Both Ashleigh and Anastasia gave their wedding vows before Triple J snatched his heart out of his chest.

When it was his turn, they both grabbed each other's arm as they listened.

"Since meeting you two, my life has been nothing less than great. Ashleigh, we met under unusual circumstances and have faced many challenges together. We've overcome them all and I'm thankful to have you in my life," he said, looking Ashleigh in the eyes. "Anastasia, Wow! You've brought so much joy to all of us with your beautiful and warm spirit. Gifting us with your love for the world. The love I have for you is everlasting beyond this lifetime," he continued locked eyes with Anastasia. "With both of you ladies I am balanced. I vow to love, provide and protect you both equally. I vow to maintain these responsibilities for the entirety of our lives being the best husband and father that I can be to our children. I love you and I'm proud to be standing here with you both today," Triple J finished causing the crowd to erupt in ceremonial cheers.

After their rings were exchanged and the three of them kissed, they moved on to the cutting of the ribbon. Triple J had the waiters pass of glasses of champagne to the adults and sprite to underage attendees.

Tapping on the glass he held, Triple J got the attention of the others as he prepared the toast.

"This all started as an idea; my wife Ashleigh came to me one morning wanting to start a farm. She didn't want a typical farm, one that raised animals and grew crops. She wanted a farm that children from the urban communities like us could learn from and gain team building, financial literacy and other skills like responsibility and discipline.

Initially, I opposed the idea. Until she persuaded me with the community benefits the farm would provide. With The Executive Homies foundation, we were able to create a curriculum that exceeds any other non-profit program available in the State of Georgia.

Watching this project come together has become an amazing sight for all of us. I ask that you raise your glasses and give honor to those who sacrificed for us to be here today and to the future," he said as he stared at the top of the barn.

Carved into a wooden plaque were the words, Dedicated to Father James Jay & Uncle Stack a Dollar.

This Shit the Realest.

Authors Letter

If you are reading this letter, I want to start by saying, Thank You so much for supporting me and this project. I've had an amazing time creating this work and I'm so grateful to finally complete this book series.

Growing up in the urban Atlanta area, the people I saw living exciting lives were, the Triple Js in my neighborhood.

"You got playas and hustlers, suckers and lames, then weird and strange. Which box you gone check off?" an OG once asked me.

I wanted to be like the players and hustlers, becoming a professional game thief soaking up all I could. A lot of it I put in the books, you better soak it up too.

When I started writing this book, I wanted my readers to get more than a book with a catchy title. I wanted to give a general view of life incarcerated, from someone incarcerated, for those who's never been incarcerated. My objective was to keep it as real as possible and discourage my younger brothers and sisters, from committing crimes because prison is no place for a player or hustler. It was made for the weird and strange.

Triple J's story is one for the history books packed with game and the only people that can't feel this is the suckers and lames, weird and strange. Now I sauced you up and it's on you to leave a player review on Amazon for ya homeboy, The Executive Homeboy. DM me on Instagram @theexecutivehomeboy I write back. We homies now, let's stay connected.

Love Always,

The Executive Homeboy

-DID YOU ENJOY THIS BOOK!
Shop with The Executive Homeboy and purchase your Shit
Just Got Real & The Executive Homies Gear @
www.theexecutivehomeboy.com

Publishers/Authors Contact:
The Executive Homeboy
www.theexecutivehomeboy.com

Excerpt for a future publishing by: The Executive Homeboy

TOO PRETTY FOR PUBLIC HOUSING

*S*ix months after her eighteenth birthday, Courtney Ja'Nae Jones was approved for her first government assistance unit in the Atlanta, Martin Street Plaza apartment complex. The exterior of her unit was poorly landscaped with red clay patches covering where grass once grew. Along with its poor landscaping, the community suffered with a high volume of drug infestation.

Martin Street Plaza apartments was a hub for one of Atlanta's largest crime family, ANW. Drug dealers used the low-income community, to get off their supply, distributing hard drugs like heroin and crack cocaine.

Although the exterior wasn't appealing to the eye, Courtney had the interior of her unit fit for a queen and her cubs.

"We may need government assistance right now, but it won't be forever," Courtney said to her twins, Cameron and Courtney as she shopped for furniture.

The twins were only two years old, but they shook their

heads in agreement, like they understood what their mother was saying.

Back in her new neighborhood, Courtney immediately became the hood gossip.

"I saw her ass from across the street. On everything shawty the baddest bih I ever seen in real life," Miko one of the neighborhood hustlers said to his boys, trying to describe the new girl that was moving in.

Courtney had natural beauty and attracted both males and females. Standing 5'3 and a half she was prettier than pretty can be. She'd always been curvaceous, with a natural coke bottle figure, but after having children her mommy spread made her an eye magnet for both males and females.

Bussing out the seem of her jeans, her hips perfectly matched her backside and while other females were getting BBL's, her ass was real.

"Say, Shawty! Let me holla at ya," Slick, the leader of The Young Crew, said chasing behind her as she walked to the bus stop.

"I'm on the move. I'll catch you on the rebound," Courtney replied, using basketball terminology after he tried taking his shot.

Courtney was young, but she was swift and had enough game to run laps around an average Joe. She was gifted in creative arts and observed attractive things with a detailed eye.

Long before Slick had spotted her, she'd spotted him. Hands down he was handsome, well-groomed with his low temp fade and deep hair waves. He dressed in the latest urban fashion, D-Boy fresh, but his street business turned her off.

As a child, Courtney had everything she wanted in life.

Both of her parents, Mario "Money-Mann" Jones and his Black and Filipino wife, Alyssa "Queen" Jones, were the streets favorite couple.

Together they moved drugs, across the State of Alabama, running up a major bag in the street. With their financial success, they spoiled their daughter, giving her everything she wanted and more.

Giving Courtney the finest things in life, the Jones's decided to move from there West End housing projects, where major crimes grew, to a safer part of Birmingham. From a two-bedroom single level apartment unit to a three-story mansion, life was good. The big transition was what her parents hustled for, a better life, but it came with unwanted attention.

Nine months after the big move, federal agents raided there home, breaching both front and rear doors simultaneously with AR styled riffles waving through the air.

"Mr. and Mrs. Jones, you both are being charged with drug conspiracy and money laundering," Courtney heard the agent say before both of her parents were thrown into the back of separate tinted SUV's.

The indictment came down quick, with several informants testifying against them. Prosecutors offered them lesser time if they agreed to corporate with the furtherance of the investigation, but both Mario and Alyssa refused to be federal rats.

The prosecution's case was well prepared and both of Courtney's parents took a plea of 396 months to avoid a federal life sentence, one the judge had no problem handing out.

33 years was a long time for them to serve, and Courtney felt it the worst. At thirteen years old, she was

forced into the Alabama foster care system, where she bounced from home to home. Sheltered by her family, she lacked certain skills like fighting but quickly learned how to thump.

"She thinks she's too pretty," the other girls in the foster home would say after they ganged against Courtney.

It was hard for the young Courtney to understand their jealousy, all she ever did was be herself. Her days in foster care were long and hard and she prayed day and night for a change.

"God please show me you're real," she asked one morning.

It was like all mighty God was listening how quick her prayer was answered.

On June 19th, 2010, the day she said the prayer, a successful married white American couple, adopted her one month before her 14th birthday.

Initially, it was the best thing a foster child could dream for, but everything changed as she aged. Courtney's body began to fill out and her foster mother Marisa, became very jealous. On several occasions, Marisa caught her husband watching the young girl's backside as she walked through the house. Insecure about herself, Marisa began to verbally and physically abuse the young Courtney, beating her to sleep once.

"You little nappy headed black bitch, I know what you're trying to do," she said while dragging Courtney by her hair. "Ya crack smoking mama should have swallowed ya retarded ass and saved all of us the trouble," she yelled while punching her.

Courtney's parents were in the streets but always taught her to respect her elders. The abuse lasted for months before Courtney finally became fed up and put an end to it once and for all.

"I don't want your man. You bald headed, white trash, bad body bully bitch." Courtney said, hitting the woman with a single closed fist punch to the jaw.

The blow was so hard, it knocked Marisa to the floor and Courtney didn't stop. Jumping on top of the woman beating her head into the floor.

Hearing the altercation, from the back yard. Max, her adopted dad ran inside separating the clawing Courtney from his wife.

Max didn't care much about the beating his wife was getting, his focus was on getting inappropriate feels on the young girl.

"Alright, alright. That's enough," he said as he grabbed Courtney by her by the breast as he separated the two of them.

While in the foster home, Courtney learned to never put her guard down after a fight. At night was when the other girls would attack the worst.

After the fight with Marisa, Courtney laid down with a bone crusher, just in case her mother wanted some get back. Surprisingly, it wasn't Marisa that came, it was her husband.

"You said you don't want me?" He asked her wobbling back and forth with slurred speech.

Courtney quickly accessed the situation and knew he didn't come to talk. She had made up in her mind that she would not be a victim to any assault especially a sexual one.

"We gone see about that," he continued snatching the cover off her body.

As the cover came off, Courtney rose quickly bashing

the iron hammer against the side of his skull. Max stared at her for a few seconds, before falling face first to the floor. Courtney watched as his body fell in slow motion and his eyes rolled to the back of his head. She didn't check to see if he was dead or alive, leaving the unconscious man on the ground. What she did know was, that the time had come for her to leave. That wasn't her home anymore.

Courtney had planned to run away when the abuse started, stacking $783 up from her hair hustle. Her bags were pre-packed with clothes and other hygiene items, enough for her to survive as a run-away.

Ready to depart for good, Courtney spat and kicked the would-be child rapist in the face before leaping out of the ajar bedroom window.

Scared and afraid, Courtney wanted to go back to the West End where her last know relatives lived. She knew that if the authorities were looking for her, that would be there first place to check so she deferred.

Sixteen years old, with $783 dollars to her name, Courtney made up her mind that she would survive on her own. She felt that a curse was over her family in Birmingham, so she hitchhiked to the city of opportunities for black people, Atlanta, Ga.

Chasing her down, Slick had finally caught up to Courtney.

"Damn, Shawty. You too good to talk to me?" He asked.

"I told you I was in a rush," she said looking down the street for the Marta bus.

"Yeah, I heard you. I just had to get a closer look at you shawty," he said looking her up and down.

"Typical nigga. Now, you got what you wanted you good?" She asked brushing him off.

"Yeah, I'm good now. Everybody calls me Slick round here. I'm out here stepping on shit," he continued bragging about his street endeavors.

"That's good for you but can you please step back. You got a lot going on and I'm not trying to get shot by ya ops when they step back," she replied to him.

"Baby you good with me," he said lifting his shirt showing the .40 Glock on his waistband. "I been staying right here my whole life. Don't nobody try me. I been getting away with bodies," he continued.

"Is that how ya mama taught you to talk to a lady. You don't know who I am and you telling me all your business. I don't wanna know about ya bodies Slick I got a lot that I'm dealing with right now," Courtney continued.

"You right Shawty. I'm tripping right now that ain't nothing to talk about and I don't know you. What I do know is that you're too pretty for public housing shawty. When I get signed, I'm gone make you mines," he said still trying to impress her.

Courtney didn't care much about what he was saying. Her mind was focused on the life developing meeting that she was headed to. She knew felt that he wasn't trying to make much of himself but agree with the one thing that he said, "You're Too Pretty for Public Housing."

Chapter 1

*A*fter getting away from the foster family and the racist state of Alabama, Courtney struggled to survive on her own. As a runaway, she was forced to drop out of school but continued to educate herself. Learning from a free online GED study guide.

"It's okay to be a fool just don't be a damn fool," Courtney remembered her mother telling her as a child.

While applying for emergency housing relief, at the government assistance office, Courtney saw a flyer for free GED testing and took down the number. She wasted no time to make the call, scheduling an appointment to take the practice test. Passing all parts on the first attempt, she was given the real test two days later and the young mother passed that to.

She immediately began her college search, looking for colleges, with the help of her education counselor and found several.

As a child Courtney loved to customize her clothes, adding and taking away from the pieces her parents purchased. Gifted in a godly way, she wished to further her talent, learning the ins and outs to fashion design.

When she received the acceptance email, for Atlanta's premier college for fashion, art and design, she immediately began jumping for joy.

"I'm going to school! I'm going to school!" She yelled in excitement.

Once she calmed and read the email in its entirety, she contacted the acceptance counselor the school had assigned to her.

"Thank you, Ms. Jones for your application. The Atlanta Institute for Design and Art's loved that you've selected us to further your education," Ms. Wanda the acceptance counselor said as she welcomed Courtney into her office. "I was looking over your paperwork and based on your income you qualify for Financial Aid and the Georgia Pell Grant. I'm sorry to tell you this, but financial aid only covers a quarter of the tuition here, so you'll need a student loan," Ms. Wanda continued getting straight to business.

"How do I do apply for that? Courtney asked.

"On the computer behind you. It only takes about 10 minutes," she continued.

Courtney filled out the forms but was denied without a co-signer. Both of her parents were incarcerated, and she refused to ever speak to her adopted parents again in life.

Damn, I wish grandma was still alive. She would have helped me, Courtney thought.

Stuck between a rock in a hard place, her worry meter began to blare.

I gotta get into school, she thought before letting off a light sigh.

"Is everything okay?" Ms. Wanda asked.

"No Ma'am. I was denied after the credit check. It said I need a co-signer." Courtney said as her head fell to the floor.

"That's not an issue. We can just ask your parents," Ms. Wanda suggested.

"Unfortunately, they're both incarcerated," Courtney replied voice filled with sadness as she cringed.

"Pick your head up girl, you in the real world now. Don't ever let anybody else's actions cause you to lower your head. I ain't here to judge you. I can't because my old man was in prison most of my childhood. And my nephew and my son locked up right now. Guess what I never let any of that stop me from getting up every morning and coming to work help good people like you," Ms. Wanda said as she walked towards Courtney placing here hand on Courtney's shoulder.

"Ms. Wanda not gone let you go out bad, young lady. It's my job to do everything I can to help you get in school and that's what I'm gone do," she said reigniting the flame inside of Courtney.

After pecking her keyboard and a few clicks, the counselor's printer started ejecting a scholarship flyer.

"The Executive Homies College Scholarship for Students with Incarcerated Parents," Courtney read off the top of the flyer. "I never knew they would have something like this," she continued.

"They didn't until my nephew, one of The Executive Homies and his buddies put their money together and created a scholarship fund after beating a Rico case. You're the only student I have here that's eligible for the scholarship. All the rest of my students either have parents outright paying their tuition or paying on their loans. You have so many reasons to be thankful because today is the last day to submit the application. School blessed because today is the last day to submit your online application. So, you know what that means, you need to start filling this out so you can get what need. School begins in three months, I'm gone make sure you have everything you need," she continued.

Courtney was so excited about school and the opportunity given to her, that she ran around Ms. Wanda's desk and hugged her. She had no idea there was a scholarship for students with incarcerated parents and quickly began working on her application.

Ms. Wanda had given Courtney a visitor pass, with a username and password for the student center. There she completed the application and 500-word essay attachment.

Eligible for a $250,000 school tuition scholarship Courtney jumped right on it.

Courtney's Essay

As a young lady growing up in Birmingham, Alabama I had a dream that I was a famous fashion designer. My dreams looked to be aligned with the universe, up until my thirteen-year-old face laid flat against the floor as federal agents raided my home.

I never knew my parents were drug dealers. They did a great job of shielding me away that part of their lives. Today I wish I had known the risk, maybe I could have convinced them that their presence was much more important than the presents.

The day I laid on that floor I lost both of my teachers, protectors and providers. It's an unexplainable pain I can never describe in words.

After losing my parents the racist State of Alabama gifted me to the foster care system. My grandmother, an U.S. Army Vet, fought to gain custody, but after several court hearings, family court denied her for unknown reasons.

Bouncing from foster home to foster home, I faced

many atrocities. From verbal and physical abuse to several sexual assault attempts, by both adult males and females. Those in authority figures.

I was bamboozled when a successful Caucasian couple found interest in me, and I was adopted into their family. I departed from them with so many negative thoughts to what they sought to adopt me for. I still they think I was meant to be their slave, especially after the years of physical and verbal abuse.

At 16 the man that adopted me tried to force himself onto me sexually, but I fought. I was able to escape the burly man's attempt and escape the horrible state of Alabama.

Hitchhiking the roads, I landed in the city known for black opportunities, Atlanta.

As a runaway, I couldn't get a legit job or apartment. I lived in different extended stay hotels, until I landed a under the table gig, cleaning rooms. It turned out to be a modern form sharecropping and the Indian hotel owner acted as the master. He knew I and several of the other girls were runaways. And threatened to notify the authorities if we refused to service the rooms for anything more than a place to stay.

I watched many of the girls survive by exchange sexual favors for other resources. I'm no better than any of them, but I refused to degrade myself and lose my virginity to a Jon.

There I did take advantage of several economic opportunity, doing hair and creating multi color beaded accessories for girls. They loved my earrings and necklaces, but my best seller was the waist beads.

Several of them mentioned to me that the waist beads

made them more attractive and the Jon's gave more when they wore them.

To be all the way honest I hated living at that hotel. The only thing good that came from there, were my twins. After being manipulated by the hotel hustler, one that reminded me of my father, I lost my virginity. I was feed so many false promises, that were so believe, about how he would help me get out of that hotel and get my own place. None of that ever happened I laugh at myself for being so naive.

Today, I'm more than thankful, for the opportunity The Executive Homies and this scholarship has given me. With both of my parents incarcerated and my last known relative deceased, I struggle to obtain a financial loan for school. Advancing my education in fashion design, puts me in the position to help another young woman, who've struggled like me.

It's my goal to become the example of what overcoming adversities look like for woman, just like The Executive Homies have done. I'm no better than any of the other applicants, but I feel I'm most qualified for this scholarship because I'm exactly what The Executive Homies mission statement says, "Outwitting the statistical Outcome."

I would like to Thank you all In Advance,

Courtney Ja'Nae Jones.

www.ingramcontent.com/pod-product-compliance
Lightning Source LLC
Chambersburg PA
CBHW012150260626
47155CB00020B/3558